# Blue Mountain Sky

### Book One
### *Smoky Mountain Mist Series*

*To my friend Barb. Love ya! Blessings. Cyn Taylor*

# CYN TAYLOR

## MRP
### Mantle Rock Publishing
www.MantleRockPublishing.com

Published by Mantle Rock Publishing
2879 Palma Road
Benton, KY 42025
www.mantlerockpublishing.com

Printed in the United States of America

ISBN 978-1-945094-03-3 Print Book
      978-1-945094-04-0 Ebook

Cover by Diane Turpin, www.dianeturpindesigns.com

# *Acknowledgements*

Love and heartfelt thanks to my sister Mary Anna who, when I questioned her about her faith and how she could be sure God existed, Jesus was His Son, and the Bible held only truth, told me this. "I would rather believe, live my faith, and risk being right, than not believe and risk being wrong; for Eternity."

Put this simply, it made perfect sense to a teenage heart and led me back to the Lord. Without my sister, my early search for God may have gone in an entirely different and most likely wrong, direction.

# Chapter One

Smoky Beauties Modeling Agency owner Brianna Walters carried a briefcase filled with paperwork and portfolios down to the edge of the water at St. Petersburg Beach. One of her late husband Grant's old sweaters stopped at her thighs. The sweater combined with cutoff jeans that barely peeked out from underneath and brown hair that flowed well below her shoulders, bespoke a look that was anything but corporate.

Bree was still trying to settle her stomach from the anxiety air travel between Knoxville and St. Pete had caused. The fleeting glimpse of a man on the plane who had reminded her of Grant hadn't helped her demeanor either. A calm morning relaxing on the beach might help remedy her psyche.

The client's photographer had already begun working with her models, so she sat down to wait until the first break. There was no reason to interrupt for introductions since he had seen fit to be on time and gotten right to work.

She was immersed in papers when a shadow blocked the sun. Looking up, she saw that the girls were on a break and the photographer had come over to introduce himself. Or so she thought.

"The girls tell me you're their manager," he began politely.

Bree always instructed her employees not to admit that she owned the company. Most people didn't believe someone so young could handle a business anyway so it did little harm in letting them assume that she only traveled with the girls as an assistant.

Without waiting for a reply, he began again, raising his voice.

"Well maybe you could talk some sense into 'em. They're holdin' me up! We've been shootin' for well over an hour and I've got very little I can use so far. They want to argue with everything I ask them to do. I say go left, they go right, I say stand, they sit. Now, I'm gettin' tired, and I would like to get a few good poses before we lose this great light. So how about you prance your useless little self over there and tell 'em how to do their job? Then I can get this over with and move on to my next shoot. Got it?"

Bree was shocked at his rude words but had a fast reply as she rose from her blanket. "Mr...?" She let her voice trail off.

He quickly filled in the blank. "Brannon," was the gruff response.

"Mr. Brannon. These young women are very capable, and I can assure you they know their job quite well. If there is a problem I'm sure we can work it out. You see, Mr. Brannon, they are accustomed to being treated with respect. I'm gathering from this conversation that perhaps you don't know the meaning of the word. I will talk to them and see what *they* say the problem is."

Brannon's look told her he didn't think she could handle herself, much less anyone else. He plopped down on the blanket she had vacated, lay back and promptly closed his eyes, ignoring, or not recognizing the sarcasm in her reply.

Bree prayed for patience with rude men as she made her way over to her models. She saw that the girls were troubled, especially Glory.

"Girls what's the problem here? Prince Charming over there tells me you are refusing his ever so polite commands."

They all began speaking at once.

"We've never worked with such a rude photographer!"

"He's asking if we don't have suits that show more skin!"

"He is insisting we meet him and some other guys for a party on the beach tonight!"

"He referred to Glory's hair as orange!"

"Okay, okay girls," Bree focused on calming them down with her words. "It does sound like he isn't the type of man most of you are accustomed to spending time with. But all of you are seasoned models. I know you've probably worked with less professional photographers before. Any chance you can get through this session and give me some time to fix the situation? I'll go back to my room and get in touch with Mr. Brannon's boss. I'll see if he can either straighten out his employee or get another photographer down here to take over. Meanwhile try to ignore his remarks. Remember, you know your true character, so it doesn't matter if he does."

At their smiles and nods Bree started back to where Brannon was still sprawled on her blanket. She was moving so quickly she accidentally kicked up some sand. It landed right in his face. He came up fast with fists flying. Had Bree been a breath slower in moving back, she would have sported a nice bruise on her left cheek.

No apology was forthcoming. Even after he saw it was her.

"You're lucky I didn't lay you flat. I've nearly killed men for less."

When Bree responded calmly, he looked a little sheepish, but only a little. "Brannon, I assure you that a few grains of sand are hardly worth killing someone over. A gentleman would have seen it as an accident. Obviously you don't fall into that category. I have spoken to the girls and though they are accustomed to a higher caliber of photographer than you appear to be," Bree placed her hands on her hips, "they have assured me that they will do their professional best to get through this shoot as quickly as possible. We have a full week of work ahead of us and it's too early for tempers to be flying. Now I suggest you get back to business before our morning is totally gone."

Gathering her things, she turned and made her way back to the motel. She didn't see the murderous glance sent her way before Brannon spun around toward the girls.

Inside her room, Bree checked her phone for the client's cell number. As she dialed she opened the drapes so she could keep an eye on the shoot. The call went straight to Vic Andrew's voice mail. Rather than leave a message, Bree hung up and tried his office number. The phone was answered after one ring.

"Vic Andrew's office. How may I help you today?"

Wow. Too bad Brannon didn't have the same manners as Andrew's secretary.

"This is Brianna Walters with Smoky Beauties Modeling Agency," she told the polite female voice on the other end. "May I speak to Vic Andrews please?"

"I am so sorry, but Mr. Andrews in unavailable until next week. Can someone else help you?"

"May I speak to Ms. Felling then? She and I have been working together."

"I must apologize again. Ms. Felling just left to attend a lunch meeting off-site. She should be back in her office by two o'clock. May I take a message for her or for Mr. Andrews? He usually checks in a couple of times a day. Or would you prefer to call back?"

Bree was frustrated that she would have to wait, but it looked like that was the only option. "Please let Ms. Felling know that we are having a few issues with the shoot in Florida and ask her to return my call as soon as she can. She has my cell number. Thank you for your help." Bree ended the call. She would have to stay in her room to wait for a call back. It would be too difficult to have a phone conversation with the ocean noise in the background. And she didn't really want to talk about Brannon where he might hear her. What she had to say was not going to be complimentary.

Knowing there was nothing more she could do until she could talk to someone at Brannon's company, Bree sat down to watch the shoot.

Things seemed to be running more smoothly. Bree refocused on the portfolios she was trying to sort through.

Soon the morning shoot was over and the girls headed back to their rooms. Bree saw Brannon leering at them as they walked away. His eyes were especially on Glory. His look made Bree want to confront him, but she decided that would be better left to Vic Andrews. She had no doubt Brannon would be reprimanded once she had spoken to his boss or to Ms. Felling.

Bree tried to focus on her paperwork, but her mind kept drifting. The problems with the day's shoot were exactly why she tried to hold all photo sessions in regional locales. She was running over what to say to Vic Andrews about Brannon when she was startled by a loud banging on her door. She made her way hesitantly across the room.

"Who is it?" she asked when she could see nothing but shoulders through the peephole.

"Vic Andrews." A very hostile voice yelled back.

Bree couldn't believe her luck. The very person she was trying to reach and here he was at her door. Bree flung open the door and was preparing her tirade when she faltered and stopped. Standing before her was the giant of a man she had spotted on the plane between Knoxville and Atlanta. He had looked so much like Grant from the back she had been close to going to him. Now his bulk filled the doorway and he was extremely furious.

Everything she wanted to say died in her throat as she compared Vic Andrews to Grant. He was the same height and build, same black hair, same dark eyes. There the resemblance stopped. While Grant was always smiling, this man was scowling. She had never seen Grant without a beard, but she was certain this man's clean shaven face could not look like Grant's. And the hair was too perfectly groomed. The nose was different, the mouth was different, and this man was a seething volcano. Grant had never shown such hostility in all the time she had known him. Bree saw then that she was being perused in much the same manner.

Andrews regained his composure first and started right into her. "My photographer tells me you are the misguided imp who manages these poor excuses for models that your boss has tried to pawn off on my company. I have commercials to organize and a narrow deadline to meet. I will not get that done at the rate he told me your girls worked this morning. He says they are sluggish, impertinent, and cannot take direction. Now, you either whip them into gear or get your boss down here to do it. I really don't care which. But get it done by the afternoon shoot or we will be re-negotiating a contract. Probably with another modeling agency."

With that he turned and was gone before Bree could utter a word. He left her wondering if his mind was as narrow as his deadline and how she could ever have thought he resembled Grant. Finally gathering her wits, she stepped into the hallway, looking left and right. There was no sign of Andrews. Bree closed the door with a loud sigh. She tried Andrews' cell again, but he was still not answering.

The time for the second session couldn't come quickly enough for Bree. She had not received a call back from Ms. Felling. Bree figured the woman had probably talked to her boss and been told he would handle the situation.

She met the girls on the beach and warned them to take no flack from Brannon. "All of you are excellent at what you do. I had a visit from Brannon's boss a while ago and I get the impression he isn't going to be much help with this situation. Were any of you aware that Vic Andrews is here in St. Pete?"

They all shook their head.

"This is the last session of the day. Try to get through it as best you can. I would still like to speak to Ms. Felling, so I'll be back in my room. I'm not that far away and can be here in a flash if you need me."

Glory spoke for the group. "I'm sure we'll be fine, Bree. Go see if you can reach Ms. Felling. Hopefully once you explain how Mr. Brannon is behaving this will be the last session we have to work with him."

The other girls assured her they could handle one more shoot. Bree spotted Brannon angling toward them and left for her room. The smug expression on his face let her know he had reported his version of the morning to Vic Andrews and thought she had been duly chastised by his boss.

Once in her room she set back to work, glancing up often to be sure Brannon had not inflicted bodily harm on one of her models. She tried Ms. Felling once again but couldn't get past the same secretary who had taken the message before.

"I am so sorry, Ms. Walters. Ms. Felling had a family emergency and had to leave before she even saw your message. Hopefully she will be back tomorrow."

Apparently Ms. Felling hadn't talked to Vic Andrews either if she had left that quickly. Bree glanced toward the beach as she spoke and saw that Brannon and Glory seemed to be having another heated discussion. She thanked the secretary quickly, dropped her phone and hurried down to the beach to investigate the problem.

Brannon was even more rude and agitated than he had been earlier. "Listen. It's the same old thing as this morning. I tell the girl to do somethin' and she don't want to do it, and I'm gettin' real tired of havin' to coax work outta these girls. Now you do somethin' with them or I will."

By the tone of his voice Bree had an idea that whips and chains would probably be his way to solve the problem. She turned towards her models. "Glory, you seem to be the one he was yelling at the most. What is it that he wants from you?"

Amanda replied before Glory could answer for herself. "Bree, he wants Glory in the water. That was not part of the agreement. It's bad enough that we couldn't shoot this back home or in the studio like we usually do but now this idiot wants to take a kid who can't swim and make her get into that rough water. He won't listen to reason."

Bree turned back to talk to Brannon, but Glory stopped her with a hand on her arm. "It's okay, Bree. I'm willing to go in the water…I really don't mind…I keep telling the others, but they aren't listening."

Bree turned to Brannon, "Why Glory in particular?"

"Look at the way the sun reflects off that orange hair this time of day. Her whole head seems to light up. With the blue of the water and that hair, well, I think I could probably get a shot that would make that girl famous."

"Her hair is auburn, Brannon." Bree had dropped the 'Mr.' once she had gained insight as to his true character. "And as much as I hate to admit it, you're right." It was all she could do not to use her hand to wipe the smirk off Brannon's face. "I do, however, forbid you to attempt to push Glory into this. She is an adult. It's her choice, and I will leave it with her."

Bree knew Glory's fear of water closely rivaled her own fear of flying. She would have no part of a scheme to get her into the water on the promise of future fame. She watched as indecision played across Glory's face.

Bree could see it in Glory's eyes the moment she made her decision.

Glory glanced hesitantly at the water. "I want to do it."

Bree didn't think Glory sounded all that confident. She decided it would be a good idea to stay with the girls for the remainder of the day's shoot.

Glory began easing slowly into the water while Bree and the other girls watched from shore. Bree sat down as close to the water as she could. She knew that if it became necessary she could be in the water in an instant.

Glory was hip deep before Brannon told her to stop and he began to line up his shots. After a while he even seemed to have Glory relaxed to the point that her fear was no longer evident. Bree knew Glory was safe in that depth unless something happened that caused her to panic. But what could happen at this point? She thought all the other girls could swim at least a little so between them they could surely handle any problem that might come up.

Bree took her eyes off Glory for a moment to look around at the colors of the sea and sky made more beautiful by the angle of the sun. Brannon was right. Glory looked amazing in these conditions. Maybe he did know what he was doing after all.

A movement to the left caught her eye. She turned to see Vic Andrews strolling down the beach toward them.

Now would be her chance. She had spent a great deal of time that afternoon going over in her mind what she would say when next they met. She was delighted it was going to be so soon. He stopped to talk to Brannon for only a moment, seemed pleased with what he heard, and headed back up the beach without even a nod in Bree's direction.

Not one to be dismissed so lightly, Bree jumped to her feet and started after him. She was still fuming from their earlier confrontation and had a few things she intended to make clear. After going only a few steps Amanda's scream along with Brannon's shout made her turn and follow their gaze to where Glory had stood only moments before. The ocean was now empty.

When Bree didn't spot her friend on the beach, she started for the water. She ran toward the place where she had last seen Glory, kicking off her shoes as she went. She jumped in and swam to the spot where Glory had been. There was no sign of her. She dove and stayed under as long as she could but there was nothing.

She looked left to right and back hoping for any sign of Glory. She wondered where Brannon was and why he wasn't helping her. The other girls might not be strong swimmers but Brannon appeared to be in good shape and should be lending a hand.

Bree spotted something on the water and headed that direction. As she got closer she saw that it was Glory. She was face down and not moving.

As Bree reached to flip her over to start for shore, strong arms pushed her gently away and lifted Glory up. Bree first thought that Brannon had finally decided to help and then realized Glory's rescuer was Vic Andrews. Of course. He would have heard the screams and shouts also.

They swam quickly side by side as he towed Glory back to the beach. When they saw that she wasn't breathing, Bree checked for a pulse. When she couldn't find one, she and Andrews began CPR. Andrews was counting as he pushed on Glory's chest and Bree alternated with mouth to mouth in between. They never made eye contact but worked to save Glory as though they had been a team for years.

The other girls stood silently, watching and praying as precious seconds ticked by. Bree glanced up only once while waiting for Andrews to finish chest compressions and saw Brannon. He had lit a cigarette and didn't even have the decency to pretend to look concerned.

Only a few minutes had passed, but Bree felt as though they worked for hours. She prayed silently that the Lord would see fit to spare Glory. With her eyes full of tears she almost missed the flutter of movement. Her breaths were shallow, but Glory was breathing. Coughing instantly followed.

Vic turned Glory to her side so she could expel the seawater. Bree saw that they were surrounded by people. Someone had called paramedics. Though they must have arrived in record time, it seemed like an eternity had passed since Andrews had carried Glory out of the ocean.

Bree and the girls huddled together as the paramedics worked on Glory while Andrews and Brannon hung in the background talking. Bree thought Andrews looked upset but couldn't hear the conversation.

When Glory was stable, the paramedics lifted her into a waiting ambulance to be transported to a nearby hospital. She had a death hold on Bree's hand. "Bree, thank you for saving me. I know this is my fault, but please forgive me for being so selfish and come with me." Bree patted her on the shoulder. "It is not your fault Glory. And I am certainly not upset with you or need to forgive anything. But I would like to speak to Mr. Andrews for just a second. He helped save your life as well. If you'll let the paramedics take you on now I'll follow in the rental as soon as I speak with him."

Glory reluctantly agreed. "But please, Bree. Come soon. I don't want to be in a strange place alone."

Glory's words reminded Bree of how young and inexperienced the model was.

It took a second promise from Bree to follow immediately to get Glory to release her grip on Bree's hand. "I promise Glory. Let me get the other girls settled and I will be right there."

Bree would keep her promise to head to the hospital soon. But first there was something to take care of.

"What happened?" She asked the remaining girls once the ambulance had driven away. Brannon and Andrews had wandered over. Bree expected the reply to come from Brannon. He didn't disappoint her.

"I told her to stop, but she kept goin' further out. I guess she couldn't hear me for the waves breakin'."

Bree doubted Brannon's story and looked to the girls for verification. Vic broke in before they had an opportunity to relay what had actually happened. "Miss, I don't know your name but we've all had a rough experience and..."

But it was Bree's turn to cut him off. "Mr. Andrews, we have already engaged in a one-sided conversation today, and I do not intend to have another." Bree knew she needed to get her anger under control. It wouldn't do to lose it in front of her employees. She started again. "First of all Mr. Andrews, thank you for your help with Glory. I appreciate you coming to her aid. Secondly, I was speaking to my girls, not to you. You could not possibly have seen what took place here since you were walking away, so I suggest you keep your mouth shut and deal with *your* employee in whatever way you think necessary while I get the girls inside and get the real story of what happened." So much for staying in control. "Whatever you decide I can tell you right now that Brannon will not be used as a photographer by this company again. I also suggest you make an appointment in Knoxville with the owner. I'm sure Ms. Walters will want to meet with you to discuss personally how we will proceed. This shoot is over and we are going home."

Chapter Two

Once Bree had hustled the girls back to her room Amanda spoke for the group. "Brannon kept pushing Glory to go into deeper water. A wave knocked her off balance and she must have panicked. We knew she had a fear of water but we didn't expect that. When she went under I guess we all kind of froze. I'm so sorry we weren't any help."

Bree reassured the girls. "If anyone is at fault here, it's Brannon, not any of you. I need to get in touch with Kathy so she can make arrangements for all of you to go home and then I need to go be with Glory. Will you all be okay if I leave?"

They all nodded as Amanda spoke. "We'll be fine, Bree. You take care of Glory and we'll see you and her when you get back home."

Bree settled the girls in their rooms and made the call to Kathy.

Her assistant voiced surprise at hearing from her boss so soon. "Hey, Bree. I didn't expect you to call. Is everything okay?"

"I think it will be. Glory is in the hospital."

At Kathy's gasp Bree briefly explained what had put her there. She only shared the most pertinent information. She wanted to keep her promise to join Glory as soon as she could.

"I'm sending the other girls home. Can you take care of the arrangements, please? I need to get to the hospital for Glory. We'll head home as soon as she is able."

Kathy asked no further questions. "Don't worry about a thing, Bree. I'll handle all of it. Give Glory my best and let her know I will be praying for her."

As she hung up the phone the thought hit Bree that she would have to deal with Vic Andrews when she was back home, and hopefully had her temper under control. She had never reneged on a contract before, but this seemed like an excellent time to start.

As soon as Bree disconnected the call, she headed to the hospital. Her plan was to fly back home with Glory as soon as the model was able. What she didn't plan was her reaction when she saw the man lounging casually against Glory's bed in the emergency ward. She thought her temper had cooled a bit. She was wrong.

"What are you doing here?" Bree asked Vic Andrews.

Andrews turned suddenly, jumping up at the angry voice and causing Glory to catch her breath. Alarms started going off and a couple of nurses rushed in. Bree ignored it all. "I asked what you are doing here. Don't you think you and Brannon have caused enough damage for one day?"

Andrews and Glory both tried to speak at once while the nurses did their best to calm their patient. "It's okay, boss. Vic is here to help." Glory was trying to diffuse the situation, but Bree was still seeing red.

Vic approached Bree, palms up as if in surrender. "I wanted to make sure Glory was really okay. And to offer my services to help arrange getting you both back to Knoxville."

Of course he did. Bree watched as Glory reached for Andrews' hand. She wondered how the two had become so chummy in such a short time. By Bree's calculations it had only been a couple of hours since they had left the beach. Glory and Vic were already on a first name basis. And a touching one.

Bree understood Andrews' interest in the model. She was beautiful, even after the ordeal she had suffered through. Glory's heart rate had finally gone back to normal. The nurses left the room with a warning to not upset their patient again.

Glory pulled up in the bed. Andrews was there instantly placing a pillow behind her back.

She gave him a grateful smile then turned pleading eyes to her boss. "Really, Bree. Everything is good here. Just talk to Vic for a few minutes and you'll understand."

Bree ignored Glory's protests and motioned Andrews outside.

As was his custom, he began speaking before they had even closed the door to Glory's room. "Again, miss, I will offer my apologies and help with whatever is needed now."

He really did look like he cared, but Bree didn't bite. "And again I say to you that we don't need your help. I'm here now, and *I* will stay with Glory until she is released." Bree closed the door behind them. "I have already arranged for our flight back in a couple of days. That should be plenty of time for Glory to be well enough to travel. If not, I'll handle that when the time comes."

"I understand." Vic took her elbow and was guiding her to a chair down the hall to continue the conversation. Bree jerked away from his touch.

"Mr. Andrews, there is nothing you can do that we need. Please leave. Glory and I will manage fine."

Vic didn't reach for her again but his dejected look spoke volumes and his words were almost pleading. "I have already arranged to pay the hospital bill. I am also taking care of any additional charges should you need to stay longer in your hotel. Glory will be moved to a private room as soon as one is available. I want to make her as comfortable as possible. I really do want to help."

Bree saw the hurt look in his eyes and almost gave in. Then she remembered Glory was in the hospital in the first place because Andrews was a poor judge of character. Instead she continued to speak her mind. "A man like Brannon should have never been chosen by you for the job he was doing today. The fault clearly lies with you."

"And I will gladly accept that."

Well, that wasn't the response Bree had expected. Maybe... no. She wanted Andrews out of their lives so she could focus. The man had an effect on her, and she would be able to think much better once he was gone. But maybe she shouldn't be quite so hard on him.

"Okay. Since you are more than willing to right this situation, I will accept your help on Glory's behalf." Bree saw relief in his eyes. "But there really is no need for you to stay in the hospital tonight. I can handle everything now. Thank you for staying with Glory until I could get here. But I'm here now, and we will both be fine." Bree turned and headed back into Glory's room, shutting the door firmly behind her.

# Chapter Three

Back with Glory, Bree received some chastising of her own. "I don't understand what's wrong with you, Bree." Glory was sitting up and looked more upset than Bree had ever seen her.

"What do you mean, Glory?"

Glory reached for her hand, urging her closer to the bed. "I know why you were upset with Brannon. We all were. He was pretty terrible. But Vic is only trying to help and from what I understand, he helped you get me out of the water." Glory squeezed her hand. "I owe the two of you my life. Equally. He has been here with me since I arrived and has been nothing but wonderful. He has offered to help me in so many ways and seems like a wonderful man. I don't understand why you, a person I have always thought of as caring and giving, would be angry at Vic."

Glory's throat sounded scratchy after her long speech. Bree offered her some water to give herself time to think before answering. She wondered if she should tell Glory about the encounter with Vic back at the hotel. That might help kill any "Knight in shining armor" thoughts Glory might be envisioning. Deep in her heart Bree knew there was more to her dislike of Vic Andrews than she was yet willing to admit openly. There was really no good reason to destroy Glory's view of him. Not until Bree had more information.

"I'm sorry, Glory. I really have no excuse to give you. Something about the man seems to grate on my nerves. I will have to meet with him when we get home anyway. I'll promise to apologize if that makes you feel better."

Glory reached up and gave her friend a hug. "Thank you, Bree. I do think he is trying to make things right. He feels guilty enough about Brannon without us making it worse. I think once you get to know him, you'll agree that he is wonderful."

Bree could see that Glory was enamored of Andrews so she took the conversation in a different direction.

"I've called your sister. She'll meet you at the airport when we get home. It sounded like she planned to bring your entire family with her."

Glory laughed at that. "She probably would, and they'd all probably want to come. I'll call Dawn before we leave here to let her know I'm going to be fine. I've already talked to my mom. I'll see everyone on Sunday for our family dinner anyway. Reminding Mom of that is how I got her to agree to let Dawn come to the airport alone. Mom always cooks a fabulous meal on Sundays." Glory looked at Bree as if she had come up with a fabulous idea. "Hey. You should join us. I've already invited Vic, and he agreed to come. Mom insisted. She wants to meet the man who saved my life."

Bree still felt that "the man" was at least partly responsible for Glory almost losing her life, but decided it wasn't profitable to bring that up again. Glory was obviously smitten.

Bree changed the topic, completely ignoring Glory's invite. There would be no sharing a table with Vic Andrews for her if she could help it. "Would you like to fly home or would you prefer I keep the rental car and drive us back? It would take a long time, but if you think riding in a car might be easier, I am happy to do that."

This was sufficient to get Glory's thoughts away from Vic. If only it had worked that well with Bree.

# Chapter Four

"Bree, come on. We have to move now!" Grant was shouting. She was trying to reach him, but every time their fingertips came close something pulled her back. It was as if ghostly hands held her in their grasp and only released their grip momentarily to tease her into thinking it was possible to make contact with her husband.

Grant was standing next to the rear door of the airplane, trying to pry it open. Bree would get close to him, and the plane would dive forward again, pulling her in a reverse path toward the front of the plane. She didn't want to go there. Bree knew without entering the cockpit that the pilot and copilot were already dead. There was nothing she or Grant could do to help them. All seats in the cabin were empty as well. She had no idea what had become of all the other passengers.

Grant finally got the door partially open, causing a change in cabin pressure that once again pulled Bree in the opposite direction. That wasn't right. The open door should be drawing her toward Grant, not away from him. He turned in her direction one last time and reached his left hand as far as he could toward her while holding on to the door with his right.

"Come on, Bree. You can make it." She could see his love for her shining in his eyes and she believed him. He had been trying to grab her hand for what seemed like hours, but this time it would work.

Bree made her way back up the aisle as quickly as she could. Her feet felt mired in mud, but when she looked down there was nothing binding her. She used the seat backs to pull herself nearer to the man she loved. She was almost there. She really was going to make it this time.

It was at that moment she realized Grant wasn't wearing a parachute. Neither was she. She had to warn him. They couldn't jump out the door without parachutes. It wasn't at all like Grant to overlook something so important.

She had just touched her hand to Grant's and was shouting to warn him about the parachute when the plane burst into flames behind him. All she could do was scream, as she watched her husband disappear into the night along with the back of the plane.

Waking from the recurring nightmare, Bree sat up so fast it made her head swim. She was gasping for breath, beads of sweat were dripping into her eyes, and her pajamas were soaked. Her cat Smoky was sitting up in his usual spot at the foot of the bed, giving her an indignant look for waking him so rudely.

The horrible dream, that had been so constant in the months immediately after she had lost Grant, had troubled her sleep less often as the years passed. Bree was sure the dream had chosen last night to return because of the incident in St. Pete with Glory, meeting Vic Andrews, and having to spend time on airplanes. Between all of that, her stress level was through the roof. Glory had chosen to fly, and they had gotten back home without incident. The flights were smooth, but Bree's stomach had still done flip flops the entire time they were on the planes.

Glory's sister Dawn had met them at the airport. She was Glory's opposite in looks with her Amazonian build and blond hair. But the two shared similar hearts. She watched as they hugged and cried as though it had been years instead of days since they had seen each other. Bree's heart turned over in her chest at the love between the sisters. For the first time in a while she felt jealousy creep in because she no longer had someone who loved her that way.

Dawn had pulled away from Glory and headed towards Bree. Before she realized what was happening, Dawn had pulled her into a firm embrace as well.

"Are you okay, Bree? I know this has been stressful for you too. I don't know what would have happened if you and Mr. Andrews hadn't been there." With this Dawn almost broke into tears again.

Since they had only been casual acquaintances, Bree was surprised by Dawn's concern for her. Especially since Bree felt she was at least partly responsible for Glory's near death experience. "I'm fine Dawn. Glory is the one to be concerned about."

Dawn gave her one more hug as their bags rotated towards them on the luggage carousel.

Once their belongings were retrieved, Dawn took on the role of mother hen. "Come on, Glory. Mom and Dad are expecting you. They are insisting you stay with them for a few days. Bree, do you have a way home? We can drop you."

"I'll be fine. I always leave my car here when I fly, which isn't that often. Just get Glory home where you can take care of her, and her family can see she is okay."

What Bree had wanted most right then was to get home and sleep for an entire day, or maybe a week. Had she realized the horrible dream was going to haunt her slumber, she wouldn't have been so quick to hit the bed.

She sure hoped the nightmare wasn't going to become a frequent visitor again. But this time it had been a bit different.

She had never gotten close enough to Grant in any of the dreams to touch him. She wondered why that had happened this time. The dream sometimes began differently, but it always ended the same way, with Grant's death. Just like in real life.

As Bree showered, her thoughts drifted back to the few wonderful years she had shared with Grant. Their love for the Lord had given them an immediate rapport from the moment they met. Grant had proposed within a few months. They had spent their honeymoon in a cabin in the Smoky Mountains and returned there often for long weekends, since their apartment in Maryville was only a few minutes' drive away. For Bree, life had been perfect. They had reveled in their time together and had begun praying seriously about starting a family when the accident happened. But Bree was not going to go there today.

Shaking off the last vestiges of sleep, she finished the shower as fast as her addled brain would allow. Once she had washed the sweat and the dream away, she dried quickly and threw on clean jeans and a top.

With the dream driven back to the far corners of her mind, her usual cheer was well on the way to returning. She felt Smoky brush against her legs as she filled the tea kettle with water and set it on the stove. The feline was one of the last gifts Grant had given her, and he held a special place in her heart. She brushed her hand across his head, and he brushed his face against her fingers. Apparently he had forgiven her for her earlier rudeness.

Bree looked down at her left thumb where it rested on Smoky's head. Grant's ring was still where he had placed it the last time they had parted.

"Here, Little Lady." Grant told her as she dropped him at the airport. He often used the pet name he had given her the day they met. He brought her close for a hard hug and kiss, and placed his wedding band on her thumb in their usual ritual when they had to be apart. "Hold this for me until I get back. It represents my heart."

Grant had given her one more kiss, told her he loved her, promised to make the trip a short one, and said he would be back within a week. But he had never come back. It was the only promise to her Grant had ever broken. Once she had determined he wasn't coming back, she had taken the ring off only long enough to wind tape around the inside so it would stay on her finger. The tape was frayed with the years of wear, but Bree didn't care. She had never removed it again, and she was pretty sure she never would.

Smoky gave her a drawn-out meow and rubbed his face against her hand. Sometimes she felt that her cat had more intimate knowledge of her true feelings than any human she knew. "You know, Smoky, it's been a while since we lost Grant. I have tried desperately since that day to understand why God took him from us."

Smoky licked her hand as though urging her to continue. She needed no encouragement. "You know there have been days I tell the Lord I understand and pray for what He wants next. And there are the ones where I barely manage to get through my usual routine until bedtime."

Bree recalled the many nights she had fallen asleep praying and crying. As the years passed, the praying seemed to have lessened more than the crying. She felt tears forming now.

A whistle from the tea kettle brought her back to the present. Bree shook her head as if that could shake off the memories. As she poured hot water over tea leaves, she decided she had barely enough time to check her garden for a late tomato before dressing for work.

As she took the steps down to the back yard, she thought of how far she had come in the four years since Grant's death. It occurred to Bree that, like it or not, she had now lived without him for about as long as she had lived with him.

Smoky accompanied her as she moved across the yard. She went "walk-about" with him through the yard and garden whenever she could. She knew he was only a cat, but it was almost as if he remembered a time when she and Grant would take short walks together outside their apartment and invite him along.

She spotted a ripe Lemon Boy tomato and plucked it off the vine. After a quick breakfast, she changed into her "corporate" suit and heels and wound her hair into a makeshift bun. It was time to move into the day. It would be her first day back after the Florida shoot. She was due to start interviewing male models today and wanted to get to the office early to prepare. Bree grabbed her briefcase, gave Smoky one last pat, and headed to work.

On the drive Bree thought back over how her relationships with men she dated after Grant had gone from bad to worse. She had been so involved in starting her business that she hadn't dated for the first two years after Grants' death. Well-meaning friends finally convinced her to "get back out there." The first few men she dated could not come close to Grant, and she never went out with them again. Many were intimidated by the fact that she was so young, yet owned her own business. Others were interested in only one thing. By the time she met Chris last spring, she had about given up on the opposite sex altogether.

One of her models convinced her to give Chris a chance. They had gotten along well until one evening right before she left for Florida. Chris had made his usual appeal toward getting Bree into bed, and she had declined. But this time was different. Chris had not wanted to take no for an answer. She shuddered to think of what could have happened.

She believed that sex without marriage was wrong. But who actually followed that rule anymore? Maybe Chris loved her and wanted to marry her but didn't know how to ask.

Four years was a long time to look for someone who obviously existed only in her imagination. Grant had been one of a kind, and she should set about finding another man and stop being so particular.

But the thought of spending the night in Chris's arms wasn't that appealing. He wasn't someone Bree could envision living with for the rest of her life. It didn't seem fair that she should have to lower her standards regardless of how unreasonably high they might be. Surely there was one more man in the world meant for her. She had prayed that night for strength to withstand temptation, but it had not been a problem. Chris had not called her since their argument.

Bree pulled her car into the garage attached to the building where she worked. Once parked, she headed for the elevator, catching a glimpse of movement out of the corner of her eye. When she turned, there was nothing there. Odd. She must be more tired than she thought. She took the elevator to her floor.

Her assistant Kathy jumped up to greet her as soon as she entered the office. "Bree, I am so sorry for all that has happened. Is Glory okay? You were pretty skimpy with the details. Can you tell me everything that happened before we start the day?"

But Bree wasn't up to discussing the details yet. "Glory is going to be fine. Can we talk about this later, Kathy? I know I must have a mountain of work waiting for me."

Kathy hesitantly agreed as she handed Bree her messages. "If that is really what you want, Bree. Maybe you'll feel up to spending a few minutes with me later and we'll catch up. Maybe over lunch?"

Bree nodded but was pretty sure she'd need more than a few minutes to catch Kathy up with all that had happened during the Florida shoot. "Could you please hold my calls so I can have a few minutes of peace to get through these messages?"

Kathy nodded. "Of course, Bree. After all, you are the boss." The last was spoken in a huff as Kathy headed back to her desk.

Bree sighed, knowing she had hurt her friend. She would have to deal with that later. She turned her attention to work.

## Chapter Five

Bree was right. An amazing amount of paperwork *had* piled up in the few days while she was gone, and her morning ended up being one meeting after another. She knew her employees had heard some of what had happened in Florida. But they didn't know the whole story, and all but Kathy were too polite to ask. That one had done nothing but hound Bree for details at every opportunity since early morning. Bree, however, was still not up to discussing it.

She felt it would be better if everyone didn't know she had lost control of the situation and almost lost an employee. That was exactly how she saw it. For the first time in years, she felt out of control. Since Vic Andrews had stormed into her life, she felt that she was on a collision course and dreaded finding out what she was going to hit and how hard. Bree closed her eyes and spoke in a whisper. "Lord, I'm sure you already know this, but once again I need to ask for patience. Would You forgive me for my quick mouth and help me to be gracious, especially when dealing with the opposite sex?"

Her mind wandered to the man who had entered her life like a cyclone last week. Vic Andrews had at first appeared to resemble Grant, but she realized now that it was only in his looks and size. Where Grant had been loving, easy-going, and carefree, this man was overbearing, unfeeling, and pig-headed. She felt her temper rising and knew she was going to get all worked up again if she didn't stop thinking of Vic Andrews. Not since Grant had a man affected her so; only with this man, the effect was the opposite of how she had felt with Grant. If only... no. She wasn't going to complete that thought. She already felt on dangerous ground emotionally with all that had happened in the past week. Thinking of Grant and what might have been was not what she needed to put her mind and heart at ease. Nor did she have time for that train of thought. Today already was and would still be a challenge. Interviewing the male models was not a task she was looking forward to.

A soft tone brought her back to the present and to Kathy's voice on the intercom. "Your first male hopeful has arrived for his interview...and...Bree...if you need any help...I'm always available."

Bree smiled as Kathy signed off. Sure she'd help. If Bree was to ask, Kathy would fly out of the office so fast she'd leave streaks on the carpet. Kathy talked a good fight, but Bree knew she was an old-fashioned girl at heart, a lot like Bree herself. They were both still searching for the right man. If there were thousands more females like her and Kathy roaming the earth, it was no wonder luck wasn't with them. There probably weren't very many wonderful, gorgeous, unattached Christian men left anymore.

The intercom summoned her again. "Bree. Are you ready to get started?"

"I'm sorry, Kathy. I can't seem to keep my mind where it needs to be this morning. Yes, please send in the first appointment."

The model sauntered into her office. Bree thought Kathy could be right. He was easy on the eyes with his wind-blown blond hair and his surfer tan. Bree decided this might not be a bad way to spend a workday after all.

Holding out her hand, Bree stood in greeting as Jeff Cahill, the first model listed on her agenda, moved across the room toward her.

He ignored her gesture as he made himself comfortable in the chair across from her desk. "I have two more interviews for commercials today, so we need to move through this at high-speed."

Once seated, he continued to wow her with his obnoxious words as the interview quickly moved into the realm of disastrous. "As you can see by my portfolio, I have the qualifications your company is looking for and there is no doubt I have the looks."

Bree was instantly angry at his claims. Then she remembered her prayer of only a few moments ago. The Lord must have decided to make her work for patience rather than granting it outright.

Calming down she took a mild approach. "Mr. Cahill. I appreciate your willingness to attend this interview. I'm sure you are very busy."

Her words seemed to be taken as an apology. "It's fine. I know you need help, and *I* am here for *you*." He gestured with his hands as he spoke, pointing first to himself, then to her.

This was not at all what she had expected, or wanted, to hear. Maybe she needed to try a different approach. "As you said, you do have the looks and the background. But I am looking for more than that. I am looking for the wow factor. Something our audience can relate to. A hidden element, if you will."

Cahill stood casually. Holding his arms out from his sides he tuned slowly, front to back to front, before resuming his seat. He smiled knowingly, as if all past jobs had been won with such simple motion. Bree gave him a moment to plead his case. Apparently he didn't see words as being necessary after that showing.

Bree did. "Okay. Well, this has been...um...educational. I have your contact info. Someone will be in touch to let you know our decision."

Without a word he stood, gave her a hand-to-eyebrow salute, and sauntered out the door in exactly the way he had entered. Bree was still laughing when Kathy buzzed in the next model.

The interviews had gone mostly downhill from there.

By the end of the day, Bree had done a complete one eighty in thinking there could be anything pleasant about interviewing men who knew they were gorgeous. Most of the models she had seen were certainly handsome men, but they all lacked something. Only a few exuded qualities that would catch a woman's attention and perhaps draw her to the product being advertised. By the end of the day, she had eliminated all but two from the ten she had interviewed.

Out of those two, only one could carry on a conversation without calling her "Baby" or asking why a woman like her would want to rot behind a desk instead of being at home making a man happy. A position many of the other male models had also expressed an interest in being the one to fill.

So she was back to her first feeling, that there weren't any good men left. Even the ones who were so stunning you shouldn't care about what was beneath the surface. Well, there was always tomorrow...and the next day...and the next.

Bree looked over her notes and sighed out loud. "Looks like finding the right male models for Smoky Beauties is going to take a lot longer than I thought."

The late afternoon sun was casting long shadows across the office as Bree stood to stretch. The movement outlined her figure against the window as the sun behind her caught the gold in her hair. She heard the click of her door opening. Thinking it was Kathy, Bree continued to gaze at the setting sun reflecting through her windows as she arched her back and stretched once again, hoping to relieve the tired muscles. At that moment, she presented a beautiful picture.

And the moment was heart-stopping when Bree realized it was Vic Andrews who had come uninvited into her domain while Kathy hovered apologetically behind him.

"I couldn't stop him," Kathy began.

In his usual boorish manner, Vic cut her off. "If you want to keep people out of your office, I suggest you get a larger secretary; although she was able to keep me waiting longer than I usually allow."

He turned to give Kathy a smile that would melt butter. "If you will excuse us, I have urgent business to discuss with Ms. Walters."

Kathy was instantly won over by Vic's sudden charm and turned to leave the room.

"Kathy, wait," Bree began, "I don't recall Mr. Andrews having..."

"You!" Vic yelled, as he really saw her for the first time. "With the light behind you, I couldn't tell who you were. I certainly don't have the time or the patience to deal with you right now. I don't know how your boss got out of this office without my seeing her, but you had better find her, and right now. I have been here all afternoon watching these... men...parade in and out of her office, so I know she's been here. Get her. Now."

The sudden change in his demeanor got Kathy's attention. She looked worried that there might be a problem after all. "Ms. Walters, should I call security?"

At Kathy's question, Vic stopped short and looked at Bree as though she had grown horns. "Ms. Walters? Brianna Walters? You aren't...you couldn't possibly be. I haven't...I mean I didn't..."

Bree was watching the changing emotions on Vic's face when she began to snicker. The snicker became full-blown laughter at his discomfiture.

"So, the great Vic Andrews does not always know everything. Am I witnessing one of the wonders of the world? Should I call in a photographer and get this on film?"

Bree's intent was to wound the man's ego, if only slightly, but Vic surprised her. He seemed ill at ease for only a moment more, then he too started to chuckle, until finally they were both doubled over with laughter. Kathy stood by giving them looks that said she was sure her boss had finally gone off the deep end. And maybe taken her visitor with her.

Vic was the first to recover enough to speak. "Well, it certainly looks as though I owe you an apology. Is there a chance we could pretend we only recently met and go from there?"

He was holding out his hand, waiting for Bree to accept his apology. Kathy hadn't moved an inch since the laughter had started, and Bree couldn't focus on what he was saying for thinking how handsome Vic was when he smiled. It was the first time she had seen him when he wasn't scowling at her or behaving like a medieval lord, and she wasn't too sure she wouldn't rather deal with the dark side of his character. He was suddenly far too charming. Bree had a feeling it would be easy to get lost in those smiling eyes, eyes so much like Grant's.

With those thoughts, she reached out hesitantly for his hand and immediately regretted it. The touch of his skin to hers sent shockwaves up her arm and down her back to settle into her very core. At that moment she knew that she would never look at Vic Andrews the same way again, and she didn't like it one little bit.

She took her hand back as quickly as she could without appearing rude. As she raised her eyes to his, she noticed that he seemed somewhat sobered by her touch as well.

Good. Could it be that she had a small percentage of the same effect on him that he had on her? Could it be that she was reading way too much into a single touch? Of course she was. This was not a man to be tampered with. This was a man who would use her up until there was nothing left. Hadn't she had a perfect display of that in the short time since they'd met?

Still, the man smiling down at her now seemed nothing like the tyrant she had thought him to be since meeting him last week. Maybe it wouldn't hurt to get to know him a little better...and they did have the matter of their contract to clear up. Her face reddened as she realized that both Kathy and Vic were watching her, waiting for her response.

"If you'll give me a chance, I'll show you how charming I can be when I choose," Vic said. He was still smiling and Bree knew she would seem petty not to accept his apology, especially with Kathy's eagle eye on them. Bree could see questions in her assistant's eyes that she was sure would be asked at a later time.

Bree gave in, motioning Vic to a chair as she spoke to Kathy. "Why don't you go on home? It's been a long day for both of us. I'm leaving as soon as Mr. Andrews and I conclude our business, which I don't expect to take that long. Enjoy your evening. We have another tiring day ahead of us tomorrow." Bree sensed Kathy's reluctance to be ushered out but convinced her she'd be perfectly safe left alone with Vic.

Moments later, with Kathy on the other side of the closed door, Bree began having second thoughts about being alone with this man who was a complete stranger to her.

As she walked around to sit behind her desk, Bree could feel Vic's eyes following her every move. When she was seated, she felt somewhat better having the desk between them. Glancing up at him, she saw that he was watching her intently. "Is something wrong, Mr. Andrews? I have been ogled by the opposite sex for most of the day, so if you don't mind, I'd like to keep this conversation impersonal and to the point."

Instead of irritating him as they should have, Bree's words caused that lazy, disarming smile to reappear. "Tell me that you sent your secretary away so we could be alone and you will make me the happiest man in town."

At that remark, Bree started up out of her chair. Vic waved her back and continued. "I'm sorry. I couldn't help a little more teasing. You are the most unusual female I've had the pleasure of meeting in a long time. You look like sugar, but you can spit vinegar. When I met you last week, I would have sworn you weren't more than a teenager. But today…today you're every inch a woman."

His eyes roamed over her, adding insult to injury. He shook his head as though he was totally baffled by her.

Bree gave him her best "I'm going to put you in your place" smile. "If you had bothered to actually meet me last week rather than yelling at me, you could have had this pleasure much sooner."

Vic opened his mouth to respond, but Bree cut him off. "You have apologized, so let's put that behind us, as you said. Now about our contract, I'm sure that under the circumstances you agree that we cannot continue to work together. I have never broken a contract before, and I don't like doing it now, but I assure you that your company will be reimbursed for any inconvenience we have caused. I'll have my attorney get all the necessary papers together and send them to you in a couple of days. After that I can be out of your hair for good."

Bree stood to indicate that as far as she was concerned, their meeting was over. Vic remained seated. "No."

"No?" Bree saw that he wasn't finished, but she continued on. "Mr. Andrews, we have had nothing but trouble in our attempt to work together. You can't possibly think that any of my models would work with Brannon now, and I certainly don't want to hinder the completion of you commercial should we not see eye to eye on other matters. No, it's better for all concerned if we part company now."

"Okay, you've had your say. Now I'll tell you how it's going to go." The Andrews mask was back. "I have no intention of trying to find another modeling agency at this late date. I still have a deadline to meet, and I can't do it without your help. Besides, I've seen the proofs from the shoot in Florida. Your girls did a great job, and I want to continue the shoot with them. Switching to another photographer is not a problem at this point, and the remainder of the shoot can be done indoors. So you see, you really have no room for objection. Our contract is firm unless I agree to let you out, and I'm expecting you to live up to your end. I had heard that your character is unquestionably honorable. That's why I chose your company. I can be happy with this arrangement and I see no reason for you not to be." Bree was wondering how a smile could have made such a difference only moments before.

Sure, she thought. He had to pick on her sense of honor. Now, she could have no reason not to agree, since he was making the concessions she had wanted without her even having to ask for them. He really did seem to be trying to work with her. "All right, Mr. Andrews. I'll honor our contract, since it appears you are leaving me little choice anyway."

"Good. Now that business is out of the way, we can move on to more important things. Like where to have dinner and how to get you to call me Vic."

"You're inviting me to dinner?"

"Of course. You do eat dinner don't you? And you probably go to lunch with clients all the time. So let's go to dinner and get to know one another better." He gave Bree his most winning smile yet. She wasn't going to be taken in that easily.

"Mr. Andrews...I..."

"Vic, please."

"All right. Vic. I don't think it's necessary for you to take me to dinner. And as for getting to know each other better... well...if you have any more personalities you've yet to unveil, I think I'm far too tired to be able to deal with them tonight."

Vic leaned forward to place his hand over hers on the desk. He seemed a bit taken aback when Bree instantly moved hers away. "You have to eat. So let's spend the time together. I'll promise to keep any alter egos put away until such a time that you are ready to meet them. I won't keep you out too late, and I really would like to get to know the fascinating woman you seem to be trying desperately to keep hidden. Or is there someone else in your life? Is that the problem? I had heard that you have been a widow for some time, so I..." Vic stopped when he saw her cringe at his choice of words. "I'm sorry if I said something wrong. I didn't mean to overstep my bounds."

Bree had to laugh at that. "Mr. Andrews, you have done nothing but overstep boundaries since we met. However, I suppose dinner with you wouldn't be totally unbearable. I'll be ready in five minutes."

Bree shook her head as she headed for her lounge. What was she getting herself into now? Why had she agreed to this? Maybe because she found Vic Andrews as fascinating as he seemed to find her?

# Chapter Six

When Bree emerged less than five minutes later, she found Vic standing behind her desk staring at something in his hand. As she drew near, she saw that he was holding the last picture she had taken of Grant right before his death.

The two of them had taken a day off to hike in the Smokies. After they climbed the Chimneys, Bree couldn't resist getting a picture of Grant. He looked even more disheveled than usual, but that did nothing to distract from his good looks.

His hair had been ruffled by the wind, and he was wearing jeans and an old flannel shirt rolled up to his elbows. It never seemed to matter what Grant was wearing. He was always devastatingly handsome in Bree's eyes. Other women always found him attractive as well. That had bothered Bree until she had finally accepted that Grant's vow to love only her was held in God's hands, and he never gave any other woman a second glance.

Vic's look was puzzled, and he was so totally absorbed that Bree was standing next to him before he noticed her approach. She reached for the picture to place it gently back on her desk.

"I didn't mean to pry, Bree. I noticed the picture when I came to the window to check out the view. This man reminds me of someone. Could it be I've met him before?"

Bree decided to overlook the casual use of her name. "Possible, but not likely. You and my husband would have been exact opposites. You look as if you live in a suit and Grant wouldn't have been caught..." Bree stopped as she realized the word she was going to use, which gave Vic an opportunity to press the point.

"So this is your husband. I've done quite a bit of traveling, and it's possible we could have run across each other. I have such a distinct feeling that I should be able to place his face. Maybe I..."

"*Was* my husband." Bree turned to look directly into Vic's eyes. He was a towering giant, but he didn't seem as menacing now as he had in their earlier confrontations. She gave him her best no-nonsense voice. "Vic, I don't know you well enough to be sharing anything about my life, or Grant's, with you. His memory has been with me more strongly than ever the last few days, and I won't help that by discussing him with you. Especially when you seem to be the cause of it. So if we're going to eat, let's go now or I may talk myself out of it."

Vic gave her a strange look and examined the picture once more but did not touch it again. "I remind you of him, don't I? We have the same hair and eyes, and probably close to the same build, but Bree, other than that we look nothing alike."

He placed his hands on Bree's shoulders and tilted her chin until she was looking into his eyes. "Look at me, Bree. Look very closely. Take your time. Examine my face. Do you really see any other features that resemble this man's?"

His hands were barely pressing on her shoulders, but Bree didn't think she could have moved away if she had wanted. Vic was as intent on her as she was on him. She did as he asked and tried to block Grant from her mind and see only Vic. He had leaned down to allow her five foot three frame better access to his face.

Of course he was right. This close Vic really looked nothing like Grant. Even if she imagined him with a beard.

Bree could feel the heat from his hands penetrating through her jacket as they stood staring at each other. Vic's hands moved slowly down her arms until he reached her fingers. He brought one of her hands to his face as if to place a kiss on the inside of her palm, but at the last second seemed to change his mind and instead placed her hand on his cheek as he reached his other hand behind her back and drew her closer.

Bree's breath caught in her throat. She knew she needed to do something to break the spell Vic was weaving around her or she would be lost. They had only recently met and he was going to kiss her. And, Lord help her, she wanted him to. As he bent his head slightly toward her, Bree noticed some tiny scars on his cheek.

"Did you have an accident?" she asked.

"What?" Vic whispered. He seemed absorbed in her nearness, and Bree didn't think the question registered.

"I asked if you had an accident. Those scars on your face, what caused them?"

The question worked better than a rebuff. Vic released her immediately and stepped back, allowing her time to get her heart rate almost back to normal.

"I also have things in my past I'd just as soon not discuss. If you're ready now, we'll go to dinner."

Vic's voice told her he had lost some of his enthusiasm for their evening together, and Bree grabbed the opportunity to back out. If he could make her feel this way after a few minutes, she didn't want to know what could happen after an entire evening.

"You know, it is getting rather late. How about a rain check?"

Vic surprised her by agreeing almost immediately. "You may be right. Tomorrow is an early day for me. I'll send someone around with a new agreement rather than have you take the time to prepare one. You can let me know at your first opportunity if all the details are in order." So it was suddenly back to business, if *she* had questions about *his* life.

"For now I can at least walk you to your car."

Bree thought of objecting to that offer, or order, but she really didn't want to go to the garage alone. It was a little frightening once the building emptied. And would probably be more so after this morning when she had imagined seeing someone who obviously wasn't there. She gathered her things, and the two of them headed out.

Vic kept a firm grip on her arm as the elevator sped them down but seemed lost in his own thoughts. Bree chastised herself for her lack of faith that the Lord would take care of her, whether in a parking garage or the arms of her current escort. She constantly longed for the relationship she once had with God, but still struggled almost daily to put her life completely back into His hands.

When they emerged in the garage, Bree thought she caught a glimpse of movement around her car, but when they reached it she could see nothing unusual.

Vic must have felt her tense up. "Is something wrong?"

Bree glanced around the garage, then back at Vic, reassuring him. "No. I thought I saw something, but I guess I'm just tired. I'll be in touch after I've read the new contract. Thank you for walking me down."

It seemed a ridiculous gesture, but Bree held her hand out anyway. After a brief pause, Vic grasped her hand and brought it to his lips. Before Bree realized what he was going to do, he was kissing her palm as she had expected him to do earlier. What she didn't expect were the shivers that ran up her spine after such a simple contact. She removed her hand quickly and climbed into her car. She drove away as fast as she dared, wondering why, if she was going to meet a man who could cause these feelings, it had to be Vic Andrews.

As she turned onto the street, she shivered once again. This time from fear. The feelings of being watched were carrying over into all aspects of her life. It was as though hostile eyes were watching her every move. She was a believer and she needed to get over these feelings of fear.

Though in the car alone, she still spoke out loud. "Lord, I know you are with me. Would you guide me safely home and take away these fears? Help me to put my trust back in You where it should be."

She arrived home as the evening sun was highlighting her mountain view, made a quick cup of tea, and carried it and Smoky's food out to the deck where she could watch the sunset. Smoky ate only a few bites before jumping into her lap for a snuggle. The feline didn't catch Bree sitting still very often and took advantage of every opportunity. She rubbed the tip of his left ear between her thumb and forefinger; one of his favorite modes of petting. He curled in against her stomach and was instantly snoozing.

Listening to Smoky purr/snore, she watched as her beloved mountains turned a beautiful lavender with the ending of the day. The sky behind was a dreamy blue with streaks of gold painted to perfection by the setting sun. If only every evening could end this way. If only Grant were here to share it. If only her life wasn't still filled with so many "if only's."

Her home phone rang, breaking her reverie. She gently placed Smoky in the chair she vacated as she rushed in to answer the call. "Hello." Nothing.

"Hello." Still no answer. There was no dial tone so Bree knew whoever had called was still there.

"It's all your fault." A raspy male voice held a threatening tone.

"What?" Bree didn't recognize the angry voice that was sending shivers up her spine.

"It's all *your* fault. But you'll *both* regret it." Now there was a dial tone.

Bree's hand shook as she replaced the phone to its cradle. She didn't understand this at all. Why would anyone threaten her? Hardly anyone had her home number or ever called her on it. She only kept a home phone since she needed it to tie in a security system. But she was still listed. If whoever this was had located her home number, he could also have her address.

She made a quick trip back outside to get Smoky. The sun was completely gone now and every shadow looked menacing. After bringing Smoky in, Bree made the rounds to her doors, making sure that each was securely locked. Then she checked the windows. She liked sleeping with them open this time of year to enjoy the cooler fall breezes. Not tonight.

Before making her way to her bedroom, she made sure the house alarm was set and locked the door that usually remained open to allow Smoky free range to her bed. Still in her clothes, she lay down and patted the bed, enticing Smoky to lie beside her. He was happy to comply. As tired as she was, Bree was sure sleep would take some time in coming. She pulled her cat as close as he would allow without protest. For the first time in her life, Bree was frightened in her own home.

# Chapter Seven

At work the next day, Bree's attorney and close friend Cal was once again trying to convince her that a merger with a local production company would be a good move. He had been pushing her to at least read the proposal for a couple of weeks now. Bree was still shaky from the phone call the night before and wasn't in her usual good humor.

"Cal, you're beginning to sound very much like a broken record. I have, I do, and I will continue to run this company very well on my own. I can't stand the thought of having someone around telling me what to do."

"That's the beauty of this proposal, Bree. No one would be telling you what to do. You would have final word on anything involving your models and all other decisions would be made mutually. The potential for development here is not something you should dismiss so lightly. A merger would lighten your work load tremendously and give you more time to pursue other activities."

"I don't want to pursue other activities, Cal. I'm very happy with my life the way it is."

Cal looked doubtful. "Bree, I don't think you've been happy for some time now. Annie and I have noticed you've been attending church less often. I thought you were finally recovering from losing Grant, but since I arrived this morning, your eyes have been on that picture more than on me. If I wasn't a happily married man, my ego would be terribly wounded."

Bree had to laugh at that but said in all seriousness, "Cal, you and Annie have been my best friends since before I lost Grant, but I will not allow you to decide when or if I am happy. I'm content with my life the way it is."

Realizing she was being cruel to a true friend, she stopped her tirade. "But...if it will make you feel better, leave the info on the merger with me, and I will at least read it through and give it some serious thought."

"That's great, Bree. You won't be sorry."

"I said I would consider it...not sign it."

"I know, but once you read the offer, I don't think you'll be able to refuse. Let's go to lunch and celebrate."

"Cal, don't you think that a celebration is a little premature? And besides, it isn't even ten o'clock yet."

"Maybe, but I'm hungry. And you know how much I hate to eat alone. Besides, who will watch my cholesterol if you don't go?"

Bree gave in, as she usually did with Cal. As they walked to the restaurant, she was thinking what a charming man he was. She would have had a much harder time after Grant's death had it not been for Cal and Annie. They had helped her through some tough times and some hard business decisions, all without once losing their sense of humor, or their belief that God had something special planned for her. She wondered if Annie knew how lucky she was.

Cal chose The Tomato Head in Market Square, one of Bree's favorite restaurants. Once they ordered, he started again with talk of the merger. "This company is a recent start-up, but the numbers look good already. I know this is a new aspect of business for you, but I think it's time you diversify a bit more."

"Really, Cal? This again? I would love to have a pleasant lunch with you. Not a business one."

"I'm sorry, Bree. You're right. I was so excited about the possibility that I got caught up. Let's start again."

But Bree was no longer listening. She had spotted a hooded figure leaning against the door to the restrooms. She couldn't make out features, but the figure was facing her way and seemed menacing all the same.

Cal brought her attention back to him.

"What is it, Bree? Are you okay?"

Bree glanced over at her friend.

"I'm fine, Cal. Do you see…"

Bree pointed toward the hallway where the figure had stood moments before. There was no one there.

"Do I see what, Bree?"

Once again Bree thought her eyes must be playing tricks on her.

"Nothing, Cal. I thought I saw someone I knew. So tell me all about Annie and the kids. What's going on in their lives these days?"

Bree spent a pleasant hour listening to Cal as he talked lovingly about his wife and their wonderful children. She almost managed it without any feelings of jealousy. And almost without once thinking about Vic Andrews and hooded figures.

By the time they parted and she headed back to work on her own, she actually did feel much better. She might consider this merger after all. It could be nice to have help with some of the tougher business decisions.

As she rounded the corner to her building, Bree felt as though someone was watching her again. The sensation was so intense, it caused her to break her step and turn suddenly, feeling as if someone was directly behind her. Of course no one was. Bree would have laughed at her own stupidity, but the feeling didn't seem at all funny or stupid.

At this time of day the street was crowded with people. Bree scanned the faces but saw no one she recognized, and certainly no one who was taking particular notice of her. She shivered as she hurried into her building. She didn't know what was causing these recent feelings of being watched, but she would definitely be more comfortable once she was back in her own office.

Once there, she was greeted by Kathy. "I hope you enjoyed your lunch/brunch with Cal. The papers from Mr. Andrews arrived while you were out. That was really fast. He must care a lot about you...I mean this contract. I put them on your desk. The messenger who brought them was sure cute, but I was hoping to see Mr. Andrews again. Don't you think he is gorgeous?"

Bree glanced at the pile of papers on Kathy's desk and replied with a smile. "What I think is that you'll be working until midnight if you don't get started on that stack of contracts. Please see that I'm not disturbed for the next couple of hours." Kathy looked crestfallen that Bree would not discuss Vic, but Bree thought that was too bad.

Although very fond of Kathy, she was also tired of all the recent interference she'd received from well-meaning friends. She had been fine on her own for years; now suddenly everyone seemed to think she was incapable of making her own decisions.

Scanning the new contract from Vic, Bree could find no fault with it, much as she tried. She signed the necessary papers and packaged them to be returned. She turned her attention to the information Cal had left about the merger. She had no enthusiasm for the project, but she had promised Cal to study it, and so she would.

She was interrupted by a knock a short time later. She saw Kathy's head peek around the door. Bree's words came out sharper than she intended. "I'm pretty sure I asked you to see that I wasn't disturbed."

"But you said two hours, and it's been over three."

Bree glanced unbelievingly at her watch. "I'm sorry Kathy. I didn't realize I had been engrossed for so long."

"No problem, Boss. Mr. Andrews is here to see you." Kathy gave her a knowing smile when Bree asked her to wait five minutes before sending him in. Bree rushed into her lounge to check her hair, clothes, and makeup, and had just made it back to her desk when Kathy opened the door to admit Vic.

When her heart started to hammer hard at the sight of him, she actually glanced down to see if movement was visible on her chest. She hoped Vic wouldn't notice her nervousness. She rose to greet him but thought better of offering another handshake. The less physical contact she had with this man, the safer she would be.

"You didn't have to come for the contract. I was going to messenger it over tomorrow."

Vic looked at her strangely for a moment as though he didn't know what she was talking about. "To be perfectly honest, I haven't thought about the contract all day."

Bree's spirits fell at that remark. Surprisingly, she found that she had hoped to have been in his thoughts as much as he had been in hers. But she perked up at his next words.

"Actually, I've thought of little else but you all day, and contracts did not enter into it. I was hoping we could have dinner tonight, so I came by early, and unannounced, so you wouldn't have time to think up excuses."

Bree blushed at that but gave him her most winning smile. "Give me five minutes." She agreed to his invitation, surprised at the words that had come out of her mouth. She paid a second unnecessary visit to her lounge to give her racing heart time to calm down; and to ask the Lord for guidance in this new relationship.

She couldn't believe Vic had thought about her most of the day. Maybe she should get to know him better. He had shown no more tendencies toward a bad temper since he had learned who she was. Could she have misjudged the man? Maybe Brannon had not explained things to him in Florida the way they had actually happened.

Vic appeared now to be courteous, kind, considerate… wait a minute…did she want a man or a Boy Scout? Oh, she definitely wanted a man. This one didn't exhibit any Christ-like qualities so far, but like all women since the beginning of time, Bree knew she could change him if given the opportunity.

"Okay, Mr. Vic Andrews," she said to the walls. "Here's your chance. Give it your best shot."

Her heart skipped a beat as she realized that she was now actually hoping for a relationship with this man. It was way too early in the game for these thoughts, and Bree immediately felt she was being unfaithful to Grant. While her mind knew her husband was dead, her heart warred with the thought that she would be committing adultery should she actually find another man she wanted to marry. Peace fell over her as she decided to dismiss such thoughts. At least for this one night. The Lord had taken Grant on to be with Him and maybe He had plans to send someone else with whom she could spend the rest of her life. Possibly this man?

When she reentered her office, Vic was lounging in her chair and looked up in surprise as she walked in. "When you say five minutes, you really do mean it, don't you?"

"You'll find I believe in promptness in all areas of my life. Don't you?"

"Absolutely, but you're only about the second *female* I've ever met who felt that way."

"Oh really? Who's the other one?"

"What?"

"The other female who is never late. Who is she?"

Vic gave her that strange look again. "I…uh…I seem to have...forgotten. I'm sure it will come to me. Are you ready?"

Bree didn't understand Vic's confusion but dismissed it as possibly the result of a tiring day.

"Is there somewhere in particular you would like to eat?" Vic asked as they walked out.

"Anywhere is fine, but I'm afraid I'll have to ask you for a ride home after. I'm having a new GPS installed in my car and they can't complete the work till tomorrow. Kathy was going to take me, but I can't ask her to wait until we get back. Would you mind?" Bree asked.

"I'd love it. That would give us even more time to get to know one another."

When Bree told Vic any restaurant was fine, she would never have guessed he would choose Grant's favorite. It was located in the heart of the university district. She and Grant had loved it for the food, but even more so for the atmosphere, especially during football season. The game day excitement was contagious. Especially with University of Tennessee fans. She kept her thoughts to herself as Vic helped her out of the car. She could do this.

Lost in her memories, she stumbled over the steps as they walked in. Only Vic's quick grasp of her arm kept her from making a fool of herself.

Misinterpreting her reaction, Vic smiled indulgently at the look on her face. "It's really not that bad. I eat here a lot and the food is great, but what I really like is the atmosphere. Football fans are great to be around in this town. Winning season or not, they love their team. Their first game is this weekend. I keep season tickets. Maybe we could go together?"

"It's not that, Vic. And you're right. We live in a great city and Tennessee football makes it even better. I'm not a snob about places like this. It's that...I...this was *our* place." Bree ended in a whisper, barely able to get the words out.

"Your place? You mean yours and...Oh, no...Bree I'm so sorry. I seem to have a hard time doing anything right with you. Come on, we'll eat somewhere else."

He turned to go back to the car, but Bree grabbed his arm. "No. We need to eat here...*I* need to eat here. It's a wonderful place, and I've not been here since Grant...I mean...I'll be fine... really." Her voice sounded a lot more sure than she actually felt.

Vic didn't look convinced but turned back around to go in, and she allowed him to lead her up the steps once again.

Bree was relieved when she saw that her old friend Charlie was still the owner. He apparently remembered her as well and was approaching them with a welcoming smile.

"Mr. and Mrs. Walters, I haven't seen you two in years. How could you forget about poor old Charlie that way? Your favorite table is available, I'll just..." he stopped suddenly as he realized that Vic wasn't Grant.

"I'm so sorry...I seem to have made a terrible mistake...I didn't mean..."

Bree took pity on her old friend. "It's okay Charlie. I guess you didn't hear. Grant passed away a few years ago. This is a business associate, Vic Andrews."

"Yes, I know Mr. Vic. I never realized before how much he resembled your husband. I guess it was seeing the two of you together."

Charlie still looked upset about his blunder as he escorted them to a table. One that *hadn't* been hers and Grant's.

When they were seated, Vic seemed a bit embarrassed about the situation as he tried to get a conversation going. "So, come here often?"

"What?"

"Oops. That sounded like a worn out pick-up line, didn't it? I meant you and your husband. Was this a place you came to a lot?"

"Why would that matter, Vic?"

"It matters because you have this haunted look on your face as if you'd seen a ghost."

Bree shook her head at that remark. "Not a ghost. Just Charlie. Seeing him reminded me of my life with Grant once again. I guess I didn't realize it would be this hard."

A server arrived with bread and took their order. The meal was excellent, but neither Vic nor Bree could keep up the conversation. The evening seemed to have been spoiled for them both.

Bree found herself casting quick glances at Vic, once again comparing his facial features to Grant's. Apparently she wasn't the only one who thought Vic and Grant looked a bit alike after all. But she had to admit that the only real similarities were the eyes, hair and build. And only when he spoke quietly did Vic's voice have a familiar timber to it.

The meal passed mostly in silence. Charlie walked them to the door as they left. "It was good to see you both. I hope you will forgive my blunder and come back again."

Bree felt bad for her old friend. "Don't worry, Charlie. You had no way of knowing." She gave him a quick hug as she assured him she would come back.

Vic remained unusually quiet as he drove her home. When he walked her to her door, Bree prepared her speech of all the reasons he couldn't kiss her goodnight. It turned out to be totally unnecessary.

"I would say I had a good time, Vic, but I think we both know that would be a lie."

Even in the soft glow of the porch light, Bree could see the hurt look on Vic's face. "Let's call it a practice date. If you promise we can try again."

That took Bree by surprise. "You want to try again?"

"Of course. If I believed in such a thing I would say the fates are conspiring against us. But I don't believe in that. So let's say until next time."

Bree nodded in agreement. "Until next time."

Vic gave her a quick peck on the cheek, gently guided her inside, and waited till he heard the click of her lock before he started back to his car.

Smoky met her at the door. She picked him up and held him under her neck for a snuggle. He purred as he always did when in her arms. If only men were this easy to satisfy. Bree watched from the window as Vic drove away.

"You know Smoky, I've only met the man. It would not have been appropriate for him to kiss me. A kiss should mean something. Not be an afterthought. We shouldn't even be hugging at this stage. Don't you agree?"

The cat gave her chin a lick then settled back to clean his paws. Smoky looked completely unimpressed with any of the reasons she had given. Nor did he seem to believe she wasn't disappointed that no kiss had been forthcoming.

# Chapter Eight

The following Saturday once again found Bree up with the sun. The weather was unseasonably warm for September. She dressed in old cut-off jeans and a sleeveless t-shirt, pulled her hair into a ponytail, and headed for her garden. Digging the potatoes was quick work since they were planted in one short tow. She put them into the wheelbarrow, washed them and rolled them to the deck to dry in the sun. Next on her list was tilling the garden to ready the soil for the next year.

She had started the hand tiller and had done one row when suddenly she was grabbed from behind and lifted off her feet. The tiller, of course, took off on its own; right toward her rose garden. Her assailant set her down just as suddenly. Vic flashed past her to save her roses as the tiller reached the edge of the bed. Bree ran over and was about to thank him for saving her roses when she realized it was entirely his fault that her flowers had even been threatened.

"Why did you sneak up on me like that?" She yelled to be heard above the noise of the tiller. "You could have caused me to faint dead away!"

"Somehow, I don't think you're the fainting type. And I didn't sneak, I yelled and yelled...practically in your ear. When you didn't hear me, I decided to get your attention another way. You must admit, it worked, and I thought the whole thing was rather funny, really, didn't you?" He was giving her a lopsided grin that seemed to dare her to contradict him. It made it very difficult to even pretend to be angry. He stopped the tiller before continuing. "Why are you doing this anyway? It's hard work for a woman."

Bree bristled at that but saw that Vic didn't mean it in a nasty way. He seemed truly concerned that she might injure herself.

"I do this because I enjoy the physical activity, I like to overcome challenges and most of all because it needs to be done and, as you know, I am the only one here to do it."

"You like challenges, huh? Okay. Here's a challenge. Let's go hiking today."

"Today?"

"Yes, today."

"With you?"

"Of course, with me."

"Now?"

"Yes, Bree. Now. Why is it you seem to have trouble with the English language when I'm around? I'm inviting you to the mountains. You pick the spot. I was planning to invite you to the UT game that's being played tonight, but I need to do something more physical. I've packed a lunch for two, you're already dressed for the part," this said while giving her attire an admiring once over, "so...I'd really like to see how you're going to get out of this one!"

That lopsided grin was back, and Bree knew she would have to think fast or risk a day in the company of a man she found frighteningly attractive, one who could probably break her heart if she wasn't careful. She had only one legitimate excuse.

"I can't leave today," she told him. "This garden has got to be tilled for the winter, and you can't tell how the weather might change this time of year."

"No problem." Vic took her by the hand, led her to a lawn chair on the deck and dared her to move. "You can supervise from here, Little Lady, and let a *man* finish the job for you."

He turned quickly, heading back to the garden, and totally missed the stricken look on Bree's face at his endearment. She didn't have time to ponder his words as she was quickly lost in just looking at Vic. He removed his shirt, his t-shirt, restarted the tiller, and was soon going at three times her speed. She watched in fascination as his muscles rippled while he worked the ground, and an unexpected longing began to gnaw at her gut.

She grudgingly admitted that he could do the job faster and probably better; and she was enjoying watching him as he did. He was certainly well built, maybe even better than Grant had been. He was tan, but Bree thought it must come from a tanning bed. A prosperous businessman wouldn't have much free time to spend outside, and those she had met before Vic didn't seem to want to take time for any outdoor activities. Still, he had invited her to the mountains to hike, and he handled the tiller as though he knew what he was doing...the muscles in his arms bulging with the effort...and had the temperature increased since she had sat down? She seemed to be perspiring almost as much as Vic.

"Dear Lord," she whispered, "please take these lustful thoughts out of my mind. If it is Your will that we start a relationship, please let me first build a friendship with this man."

Vic finished far too soon, and Bree tried to avert her eyes before he caught her staring.

As he approached her, she could tell by his lopsided grin that she hadn't quite managed to look away in time. He picked up his shirts but didn't bother to put either back on as he came up onto the deck and knelt in front of her. It took all of Bree's self-control not to reach for him. His skin glistened with a light sheen of sweat, and his hair had fallen over his forehead, giving him a rakish appearance Bree found hard to resist.

Vic looked longingly into her eyes as he asked, "What would a hard-working man have to do to get a cold drink and a hot shower around here? I'd be willing to pay almost any price."

His intentions were clear. Bree tried to reply, but his mouth, only inches away from hers, made coherent thoughts difficult and speech impossible. She would only have to lean forward ever so slightly to touch her lips to his. He was so close she was sure she could hear his heart beating...or was it hers? Vic was giving her the choice. He hadn't moved a muscle. It would be so easy.

Suddenly, he yelled and jumped away from her. She was so dazed by her feelings it took a moment to figure out what had happened. She saw Smoky at the same time Vic did. The feline had come up between them and must have rubbed against Vic's legs. Vic picked him up and tucked the cat under his chin.

"Be careful, Vic, he doesn't like strangers, and I'm the only one he'll let pick him up."

Bree reached for Smoky, but she was too late. The traitor had already snuggled in and was purring loudly into Vic's neck, totally content on his high perch.

"You must have this cat confused with another one. I get along great with animals and this one is obviously no different," Vic replied, stroking the cat's fur.

Hard as it was to believe, Vic was right. Smoky acted as though he had known the man all of his life.

Bree gave Vic a daring look as she took Smoky from his arms anyway. "You'll find a shower through the back door in the utility room. Towels are on the shelf and cold drinks are in the fridge. You want to hike? Fine. Be ready in ten minutes, and we'll do the Chimneys. Think you can handle that, city boy?"

Bree knew Vic wouldn't understand why she sounded so angry, because she wasn't sure herself; and she fully expected him to change his mind about spending the day with someone so changeable, but he surprised her once again.

"Great. I've not been there yet this year. I'll be ready in a jiff."

Bree found herself doing Kathy's open-mouthed pose as Vic disappeared through her back door. And she had to wonder what he meant by "this year."

"Traitor," she said aloud to her cat once Vic had vanished inside. Smoky gave her his best "Who me?" look and what was most definitely an all-knowing smile before Bree headed in to grab gear for the day.

# Chapter Nine

Bree spent the drive into the Smokies finding out more about Vic, or at least trying to. Getting him to talk about himself was harder than holding Smoky still for a flea treatment.

When he did share some info it was brief. "I grew up around here. Love the mountains. Started my own business about three years ago. I have a few small companies that have become somewhat successful. I looked into your company when I needed models."

He was stingy with information about his background. What he had shared so far explained his knowledge of her past and present and was beginning to shed some light on his enjoyment of hiking in the mountains. Bree had miscalculated when she had assumed he was more at home in the big city. She hadn't yet found the proper moment to ask Vic if he was a Christian, but she knew the Lord would make time for that if the relationship was to grow. Bree might have lost some of her devotion during the years of living without Grant, but a relationship with a non-believer was out of the question for her.

In spite of herself Bree cringed as they drove past the airport where she had last seen Grant. Fortunately, Vic didn't seem to notice, or so she thought.

"So, tell me more about this ghost that stands between us. He must have been some man to still exist for you after all these years."

"That's a rather callous choice of words, Vic. And I really don't see the need to tell you any more than you already know. I thought maybe we could spend a pleasant day together. Do some hiking. Maybe get to know each other a little better. But that does not include answering questions about my husband. I can't understand why you would want to know about someone who now exists only in my past. Why are you so interested?"

"I'm not...not really. I just get the feeling that he's still very much a part of your present. Especially since you referred to him as your husband. I can deal with fighting for your attentions if I can see my competition, but with you, I seem to keep coming up second to a memory."

Bree could feel her agitation rising with Vic's remarks but if she was honest with herself, she would have to admit that he had a point.

"Okay, Vic. Suppose I do my best to keep the past in the past...for today...and you do your best to open up about yours a little more. You already know quite a bit about me from your research before we started doing business together, and that doesn't seem fair. What do you say? Do we have a deal?"

"Sounds like a good plan to me. Let's give it a try. I'll start by showing you my future home in the mountains. The house is only partially complete, but you can use your imagination. It's on Little Round Top overlooking Wears Valley. The view is great. I haven't been there since all the recent rains. I'd like to see if any damage has been done. The road isn't paved yet, but I'm sure we can manage. It's very secluded and undeveloped, but I'm sure you're going to love it. It could mean missing our hike to the Chimneys, but we could always do that another day. I didn't bring my gate keys since I didn't plan to come here this weekend, but maybe some of the contractors are still there working and the gate will be open. What do you say?"

He sounded to Bree like a little boy who wanted someone to love his new toy as much as he did. It was the most words she had heard him use without a pause.

"Okay, okay. We'll go there first. You convinced me. But I warn you, at the first sign of a wild boar, I turn back."

Vic laughed as he casually slipped his arm around Bree's shoulders and squeezed playfully. She thought he would remove his arm quickly, but when he didn't, she decided that it wasn't half bad having that extra weight on her shoulders. No, it was actually rather comforting, maybe too comforting…

"Here we are." At the sound of Vic's voice, Bree jumped, dislodging Vic's arm from her shoulders, causing him to send the car toward the ditch beside the road. Vic recovered quickly and gave her a sharp look.

"Wow! You're skittish when you first wake up, aren't you?"

"I was not asleep."

"Oh, really. I suppose the music I've been hearing for the last ten miles wasn't you snoring, either."

"I do not snore. And no gentleman would ever…" Bree stopped when she saw that lopsided grin that she was coming to know too well, realizing she was being teased. "Shame on you, Vic." But she was grinning now, too.

Vic turned off the paved highway, drove through an open gate and onto a dirt and gravel road that didn't appear large enough for even one small car to travel, much less the SUV Vic was driving. The mountains towered on one side and on the other was a sheer drop, straight down to the river. Bree was afraid to ask what would happen if they met another vehicle.

"Hey, don't look so scared. I've driven this road a lot," Vic told her, as they bounced and hopped over rocks and ditches. "Trust me, I can handle it."

"I'm not scared," Bree told him indignantly. Even though she was a little nervous, she'd never admit that to Vic. She knew he had glanced over at her, but she had her eyes glued to the road ahead and therefore was the first to see a problem. "But, how are you going to handle that?"

Vic turned from her and saw that the rains had indeed done some damage. The section of the road ahead was almost completely washed out leaving the mountainside as it had once been, minus a few trees and bushes. Vic was not to be out-done.

"No problem. We'll walk. It's not that much further. I can leave the car here. Obviously no one else is going to need to get past this point today." Did he sound a little too happy about that? "We may have company at the house if the workers got here before this happened. There is no other way in or out. Can you handle a vertical climb?"

"I can if you can, city boy!"

Vic looked doubtful, but rather than voice an opinion, he grabbed some of their gear and started up the steep hill. Turning back after a short distance he looked surprised when she was right on his heels. Her business had kept her very busy, but she never let her physical ability diminish. She had always found time to visit her beloved mountains and keep her climbing skills up to date.

The climb was steep enough that talking was difficult, so they hiked in silence. After about twenty minutes they reached a summit and Vic turned to see if she needed help. Bree could tell by the look on his face he was surprised that she was still right behind him and not even breathing hard. But he also looked pleased. He didn't comment but led her around a bend and up to a house that Bree immediately fell in love with, even before seeing the inside.

It was her house. On the heels of that thought came another; that this being her house was a stupid thing to think. But it was almost identical to the house that Grant had designed and was going to build for her as soon as they could afford it. But, of course, that and many other dreams had been dashed years ago. The afternoon sun hitting the blue metal roof created a halo around a beautiful log cabin. The cabin faced east, had a vast porch which completely encircled it, and giant, well-placed windows that would let the sun in from all sides. The total picture left her breathless.

"Vic, it's absolutely beautiful. I love it. Did you design it?"

Vic looked sheepish but very proud. "Yes, I did. I love having the sun coming in at all times of the day, and I like sitting outside when it rains without getting wet, so the full porch is great. There are other nice features, but you'll have to come inside to see them. As I said, I didn't bring my keys, but we don't usually lock the doors. Access to this area isn't too easy as you can see, especially today, and most people don't ever think about driving to the top of this mountain. It's a very safe and secure place. Since the gate was open, I thought some of the workers might still be here, but I guess they left before the wash out and forgot to lock the gate. I'll have to talk to them about that."

Vic opened the front door and ushered Bree in. Again, she was awestruck. The foyer led into a large room with a pass-through fireplace that took up most of the center of the room. A totally modern yet rustic-looking kitchen was off to the right and the bedroom was to the left, with no divisions between other than the fireplace.

"Looks as though you plan to remain a bachelor all your life," Bree commented.

Vic looked around his house with a hurt expression before asking, "Why do you say that? Don't you think there is a woman who would like my design?"

"Oh, no, Vic I didn't mean anything like that. Your home is beautiful. I was wondering about the lack of privacy. This is fine for one person, but it might get to be a little too much togetherness for two, with only one main room and a bath. There is a bath, isn't there? No little buildings hovering around out back are there? That would be asking a little much of even the most liberated female." Bree thought the house would have been perfect for her and Grant but couldn't imagine living in such close quarters with another man.

"Of course there is a bathroom inside, and as for the other, I guess I never really thought about sharing this place with anyone else. There hasn't been anyone since…" Vic seemed unable to complete the thought. "Well, if the time ever comes, I'm sure I could make modifications."

"Still," Bree acknowledged, wondering who Vic's anyone was, "it would be a shame to change anything about the house. It really is perfect just as it is."

"Come look at this." Vic sounded as excited as a child as he pushed her toward one of the windows. Bree caught her breath when she saw the view. Even with her frequent trips to the mountains, she didn't think she would ever get used to their beauty. The house overlooked Wear's Valley as Vic had promised. What he had not mentioned was the angle of the view and how he had turned the house to take the best advantage of that. The sun was beginning to cast longer shadows as morning turned to afternoon and with the fall colors starting to appear, it was a picture only God could have painted. Bree hugged herself from the sheer joy of the beauty and was turning to brag to Vic about God's handiwork when she sensed him behind her. He moved closer and wrapped his arms around hers, pulling her back until she was leaning against him with her head on his chest.

"Isn't it the most beautiful thing you've ever seen?" he whispered in her ear.

Bree thought that it was but could only nod her agreement. Her throat had gone completely dry and seemed to have closed up as well. Vic moved his hands up to her head and began a slow, sensuous massage with his fingertips while he moved her hair away to give himself access to the back and side of her neck. Bree closed her eyes and thought how good it was to be in Grant's arms.

Whoa. Where did that come from? The feelings were very familiar, but the man who was turning her to face him was not Grant. Vic looked into her eyes, studying her for only a moment before, with a low groan, he leaned down to lightly touch his lips to hers. His kiss was so soft and brief, Bree wasn't sure he had touched her at all. When she opened her eyes Vic was looking at her with an expression that held not only the beginnings of passion but something more. Wonder? Surprise? Bree wasn't sure.

What she was sure of was that she needed to get out of this secluded place and fast. "Vic, it is very beautiful here, but if we don't go now, we won't make our hike today."

"I know." But he didn't move. "Bree have we met before? I got the most unusual feeling just now when we kissed."

"Yes, Vic. At my house, this morning, remember? And in Florida before that..."

"No, Bree, I'm serious. Before Florida... had you ever seen me before? And the way you smell. It's somehow so very familiar."

He had such a serious look on his face, Bree decided not to tease him and reluctantly admitted to her mistake on the plane.

Vic wasn't convinced. "But, I didn't see you on the plane, and I feel...more...more than a quick meeting, as though I've not only known you but...touched you...as we touched just now. I feel as though I already know every curve and plane of your body without having done anything more than kiss you. And I'm sure I recognize that scent."

The conversation was giving her unusual sensations, too, and Vic was using that low, seductive tone of voice again, the one so much like Grant's.

Reluctantly, Bree pulled away. "Vic, I'm pretty sure we have never met before Florida. I think I would remember. As for the way I smell, I created a line of body lotions a few years back. Grant's favorite was always lavender. It became my favorite as well. I've been wearing it and selling it for years. A lot of other women probably wear the same scent. See. A reasonable explanation. Now we really do have to go or else forget about our hike for today."

"I'm sorry, Bree. You're right, of course. It's that, for a moment there, everything about you seemed so... familiar. Come on, we'll start back."

The trip down was made in what had to be record time and with even less conversation than the trip up. Vic helped Bree into the car and began slowly backing down to the gate since there was no place to turn around. As they made the last bend in the road, Bree was lost in confusing thoughts that were interrupted by Vic's sudden shout.

"Oh, no! This can't be happening!"

"What, Vic? What is it?" Bree followed Vic's gaze and could not believe what she was seeing. The gate that had been wide open when they arrived, and their only outlet to the main road, was now securely padlocked.

"So…unlock it," Bree stated calmly.

"I can't. Remember? I told you I left my keys at home. One of the boys must have realized he forgot to lock the gate and come back."

"So, what do we do now?"

"Well, as I see it we have a few choices."

"And those are?"

"I can bust down the gate with my vehicle."

"A little extreme, don't you think? What else?"

"We can try our cell phones to see if we can get reception up here. I usually can't, but you never know."

They both took out their phones, but neither could get a signal.

"Next?" Bree questioned.

"I can start walking to the nearest house, hope they have a working phone, and call one of the guys who lives close and has a key."

"How far is that walk?"

"Five miles, maybe more."

"Doesn't seem practical. Do you have any other ideas?"

"Well, we could hike back up to the cabin and spend the night. The guys will be working early tomorrow even though it's Sunday because the house is so near finished, and they obviously know they'll have to get someone up here to repair the road. I packed enough food so we should have plenty to eat, and I can build a fire to keep the house warm enough..." Vic's voice trailed off as he realized their situation sounded very much like the old "Sorry, but I've run out of gas routine."

Bree believed him. And if she had to admit the truth, she was having a wonderful day with him. "Okay."

Vic was completely taken off guard by Bree's ready agreement. "Okay? Just like that? No demands? No accusations? Just, okay?"

"Vic, I'm used to roughing it in these mountains and your accommodations offer a great deal more than I've had on many occasions. I can't believe this was all some ruse of yours to get me alone. Even *you* wouldn't go so far as to destroy your own road, so I see no problem with spending one night. Do you?"

Vic shook his head as he put the car in gear to head as far as they could back up the mountain. "You know, Bree, you aren't like anyone I've ever known. Just when I think I've figured you out, you do something totally out of character. Your reactions are never what I expect."

"Good. That ought to keep you on your toes around me. By the way, who has to carry that giant picnic basket up the mountain?"

"How about I flip you for it?'

"I don't think so. How about if I carry the blankets and you can wrestle with the basket?"

"You're a mean woman, Bree," Vic groaned.

"Oh, you haven't seen anything yet." Bree grabbed the blankets the instant Vic stopped the car, jumped out, and headed back up the mountain before he could get a chance to question her about her last statement. She suspected she was going to have a lot of repenting to do when tomorrow came, but she couldn't bring herself to worry about that now. After all, what choice did she have? She was certainly strong enough to resist this man, no matter how attractive he was. Wasn't she? A familiar Bible verse about putting yourself in sin's way came to mind, but Bree dismissed it as quickly as it came.

# Chapter Ten

The walk back up took longer than before as they were both a bit tired from the first trek. As they neared the cabin, Vic gave her a playful slap on the rear.

"Okay, Woman, fix me some grub. I'll go gather some wood."

Vic was being cheerful, but Bree wasn't feeling nearly as brave as she had let on back in the car. Suddenly, the prospect of being alone all night with Vic seemed like a very bad idea. If he touched her again in an intimate way, she wasn't sure if she'd be able to make him stop, or even if she'd want him to.

By the time Vic returned with firewood Bree had placed the food on the blanket so they could face the window overlooking the valley. She had gone outside and hurriedly gathered some fall blooming wildflowers. Finding an empty paint can, she had placed the flowers in that and added some water from a gallon jug she had found in the incomplete kitchen.

"I had no idea you were so domesticated," Vic crooned on his return.

"There's quite a lot you don't know about me, Vic. How about getting that fire going before we eat. These clothes would have been fine for hiking, but the later it gets, the colder I get."

Vic was immediately contrite. "I'm sorry, Bree, I hadn't thought about that. Here."

Vic pulled off his flannel shirt, leaving himself in his t-shirt, but the cold didn't seem to affect him. He wrapped the shirt around her shoulders and once again she was taken back to thoughts of Grant. The shirt was still warm from Vic's body and smelled of him; a clean, woodsy scent so much like Grant that Bree's knees shook when Vic's fingers lightly brushed her shoulders. Did he feel that too? Apparently not. Seemingly unaffected by her reaction to his touch, Vic turned back to build the fire. Bree watched the muscles ripple in his back and took the time to study Vic more closely. He had fine, chiseled features that would set any woman's heart to fluttering, hers included. But his mannerisms and overall looks still favored Grant enough that until she could conquer that comparison, Bree couldn't let herself think of Vic as a romantic possibility, and she was pretty sure he felt the same.

Vic got the fire going. As it began to burn higher, Bree thought again of the tiny scars on Vic's face. Maybe now would be a good time to ask about those again. Vic seemed more approachable here in this mountain setting, nothing like the business baron he appeared to be when they were in the city. He glanced up at her and smiled. He was obviously happy about the way the weekend was going and in a good mood. Bree decided not to spoil the moment.

"Bree, in case you're wondering, I really didn't plan on things happening this way. An overnight kidnapping never entered my mind. Not that I'm unhappy with how things have turned out, but really, I…"

"I don't doubt your sincerity, Vic," Bree interrupted. "I have come to know you better today and feel perfectly safe in your company." There. That ought to keep him on his honor.

Vic rose from the fire and came to stand directly in front of her. He grasped her hands and pulled her toward him, pausing a moment as he looked deeply into her eyes before he said, "I'm starved. Let's eat."

Bree once again found she was both disappointed and relieved when Vic moved away.

He cut her a piece of bread and some cheese, but she stopped him as he offered to open a bottle of wine he'd brought.

"This is becoming a little too poetic for me. I think I'll pass on the wine."

Vic laughed, that deep, throaty bear of a laugh that Bree had only heard a couple of times. The one so much like Grant's.

"Come to think of it, I don't really like wine either, but I thought you might. I should have probably known better. Maybe if I plan everything the opposite of what I think you want, I can learn how to please you. Bree, I have to tell you...I don't remember when I have enjoyed myself as much as I have the few times we've been together. It's been years since I've laughed so much or felt as happy as I do at this moment. I am so glad to have this uninterrupted time with you."

Bree suddenly felt the need to lighten the mood. Setting her food down, she challenged Vic. "Okay buddy, you've got me stranded. There is nowhere I can run so go ahead and admit it. This was all an elaborate scheme to keep me from showing you up on the hike. You knew the road was out and you never intended to get any further than this cabin, did you?"

Bree had jumped up and was pacing in front of Vic with her hands on her hips and fire in her eyes, looking as though she was really as angry as she sounded.

Vic rose also and approached her with his hands out, imploring her not to think that of him, "No Bree...I wouldn't...I couldn't ever. I have come to think much too highly of you to try and trick you like that. I have the greatest respect for you and think I may even..." Vic stopped before completing the sentence, apparently realizing what he had been about to admit to this woman he barely knew. Bree could no longer hold in her laughter and didn't catch his last words.

Realizing he had been played, Vic jumped toward Bree as she vaulted around the fireplace trying to escape his grasp; but Vic was too quick for her. He grabbed the shirt he had loaned her, spinning her around. The motion caused them both to lose their balance. Vic twisted as they fell to the floor so that Bree landed on top of him and he could take the brunt of their fall. Bree felt and heard the air whoosh from his lungs as she fell hard on his chest. She tried to be serious as she asked if he was hurt, but she couldn't seem to get her laughter under control. She hadn't laughed like this in years.

Vic pretended not to share her amusement and scolded her between gasps. "Woman, I'm dying here and all you can do is laugh. What do you think is so funny?"

He was complaining, yet his hold on her was so tight Bree could not have risen if she had wanted to; and she really didn't want to.

"Oh, Vic, you may be bruised tomorrow, but I hardly think you're dying. If you'll let me up I'm sure you'll catch your breath and recover much more quickly."

"Are you kidding? I risked life and limb to get you here. I think I like you just where you are. Or maybe..."

Before she knew what was happening, Bree found their positions switched with Vic looming over her. He seemed fully recovered now and was careful not to let his full weight rest on her.

"I hit my head on the floor," Vic told her. "I'm pretty sure I'll have a bruise on my forehead. How about a kiss to make it better?"

He wasn't pushing, but Bree knew he was waiting expectantly, not quite knowing what her response might be. What kind of new game was he playing now?

Suddenly nervous, Bree told him, "Vic I'm sure you'll heal quite nicely without my help, so if you'll let me up I promise to behave and not tease you anymore today."

Bree's eyes were pleading with his, but Vic wasn't giving in that easily. "I don't think you're in much of a bargaining position, Little Lady."

"Vic, this isn't funny anymore." His endearment caused her to turn away so he wouldn't see her stunned look.

"No. It isn't. It isn't funny at all."

Vic had become less concerned now with keeping his weight off of her. Bree could feel every inch of his body where it pressed into hers. She could also tell that he didn't need any more encouragement from her to be truly enjoying himself. Still...one little kiss...just on the forehead...what could be so bad about that? The daylight was beginning to fade as Bree studied Vic's face, wondering again at the tiny, almost invisible scars. Should she allow this man into her heart? Could she?

Vic waited quietly, watching Bree's face as she warred with her emotions, giving her time to decide. Making her decision, Bree reached up and pulled his head down just enough so she could place a very chaste kiss on his forehead. His skin felt warm and ...soft? She hadn't expected that.

Vic pulled back and pointed to his chin, "I have a slight ache here. I think your head must have hit me when we fell."

Bree made no comment as she again reached for his head to kiss his chin. It was scratchy with the day's growth of beard. She felt warm all over and was pretty sure it wasn't from the heat of the fireplace. Vic hesitated only slightly as he pulled back once more to point to his lips. Bree could read the question in his eyes and knew there would be no turning back from this choice she was about to make. Their bodies were pressed too tightly together for her not to know what this exchange was doing to Vic's composure, yet he was giving her every opportunity to pull away if she chose. She didn't. Bree concentrated on the tiny scars on Vic's face as she reached for him once more. As she brushed her lips against his, she tried to empty her mind of all thoughts except those about Vic. She almost made it, too.

Her conscience now conflicted with other feelings, telling her she needed to stop, but Bree wasn't taking advice from any direction. Vic increased the pressure on her lips as he brought one hand up to her face. He pulled back slightly but only to nibble at her lips before he began an assault on them that Bree knew was going to drive her crazy if he didn't stop, yet she hoped he wouldn't.

With courage she didn't know she had, she moved her hands from his head down his back and to his waist. She heard his sharp intake of breath as he groaned her name and kissed her in earnest once more. Bree breathed out Vic's name in between kisses. Or so she thought. It wasn't until Vic suddenly jumped up and reached down to help her that Bree realized what she had done.

As she struggled to get her breathing back to normal she tried to apologize.

"Vic I can't believe I did that…I don't know what to say… how to apologize…I thought I had blocked Grant from my mind…you seem so much alike. No one has affected me like this since Grant. We were together four wonderful years, and I still struggle to let go…but to call you by his name…" she faltered, knowing there wasn't going to be a good way out of this blunder.

Bree couldn't bear the hurt look on Vic's face anymore, so she walked to one of the windows and stared out at the ridge where the sun was beginning to set. She heard Vic behind her banging things around, probably cleaning up their picnic. She had certainly lost her appetite, and he probably had as well.

How could she have been so thoughtless? Why had the Lord taken Grant away only to bring a man into her life after all this time who reminded her so much of him?

*For I know the plans I have for you, saith the Lord; plans to prosper you and not to harm you, plans to give you hope and a future.* Funny that that verse should spring to mind right now.

"Okay, Lord, I was definitely moving into sin, and You sure took care of that, didn't You? I'll bet I won't have to worry about getting into this situation anymore. Once Vic gets me back to Knoxville, he'll probably never speak to me again."

But he was speaking to her now.

"Bree, come here."

She didn't want to turn around for fear of what awaited her, but she couldn't stand and look out the window all night.

"Lord," she prayed silently, "help me to make amends and get through this night. With Your help I'll try to keep my lustful thoughts off of Vic, and stop thinking about Grant. Maybe when I get home You and I can have a one-on-one and You can straighten me out. I really want to have the relationship I once had with You. Please help me to get that back. Please forgive me for what I've done tonight...and for what I wanted to do."

Bree turned to face Vic and was completely overcome by what she saw. Vic had pulled two sawhorses together and placed a sheet of plywood on them. He had put the food in the center of the plywood and was standing on the other side looking quite pleased with himself.

"Does this look safe enough? If you will notice, I have strategically placed the food directly between us. I promise not to attack you again...at least not until you've eaten and regained your strength. Give me another chance? Maybe you would even feel safe enough to tell me how often you have these little conversations with yourself?"

Bree had only thought she had been silent in her prayer. "I wasn't talking to myself. I was talking to God, but I doubt He wants to hear anything I have to say right now."

"God is always ready to hear us when His children seek Him," Vic told her, yet he looked surprised at the words that had come out of his mouth.

"Vic, you amaze me. When we first met, you were enraged over a seemingly trivial misunderstanding and now, when you have a good reason to be angry with me, you respond like this. And what you said about God, where did that come from anyway? I'm afraid I don't understand you at all."

"What's to understand? I only *thought* I had a reason to be angry when we first met in Florida. Anyway, that was business and this is personal. I think you are well on your way to becoming very special to me and I won't let you put me off by calling me by another man's name. As for the thing with God...I haven't thought about God in a long time...or maybe ever...but since you came into my life, I have these feelings I can't really explain...feelings of knowing Him...of something I should remember..."

"But, Vic..."

"No Bree, no more. Enough talk for now. We seem to get into trouble when we talk, or touch. If you have your appetite back, come and eat and we'll watch the sun go down over the mountains. I can personally guarantee one of the most beautiful sunsets you've ever seen."

Vic was right. As they ate, in quiet this time, the sun disappeared behind the mountains and there were just enough wispy clouds to make a gorgeous display of light and color.

Bree loved to watch the sun rise, but she had to admit that this moment in time rivaled any mornings she had spent recently. When they finished eating, Vic moved around to her side of the table, pulled her down to the floor, and sat her between his knees. Bree held her breath, waiting to see if he would honor his word, but he did no more than wrap his arms around her and hold her gently. She was grateful for that. She wasn't sure her heart could take much more in one day.

"So, tell me what it's like owning your own modeling agency."

Now why would he care about that? But it did seem like a safe topic. Still, she hesitated.

"Oh, I'm sure I would bore you with that information," Bree said. "What possible interest could you have in that aspect of my life?"

"Don't underestimate me, Bree. I'm interested in everything you do, every thought you have. I want to get to know the real Brianna Walters."

Reluctantly, Bree told him her real reason. "I always wanted to be a model, but my body wouldn't comply."

Vic gave her a look that said he found no fault at all with her body. She ignored him.

"I decided to take business courses so I could one day own my own company." Bree thought back to the reason she was able to do that. "The opportunity came much sooner than I expected. I know you don't like hearing Grant's name, but if he hadn't died, I would never have had money to start my own business. Since I couldn't be a model, I decided owning an agency, something Knoxville didn't have when I started, would be the next best thing. And here I am, a few years later with a very successful modeling agency."

Bree was enjoying having a man to share her story with and who seemed intent on listening. For that reason she also told him about the proposed merger. "My attorney thinks it would be a good idea for me to consider this, but I'm very leery of allowing anyone to have a say in my business. On the other hand, it might be nice to have help when there are difficult decisions to make. I don't know. I think I should maybe meet the owner of the other business before I make my decision...that might help me make up my mind. You're a business owner. What do you think?"

Vic seemed uncomfortable with her question. "I think this should be entirely up to you. No one should influence you either way. You've made your own decisions for years; I'm sure you'll make the right one now."

Bree wasn't so sure of that. "Tell me about your business, Vic. What's it like being in charge of major productions?"

Vic chuckled at that. "I'm afraid none of my companies are involved in major productions. We do small-time only. Major productions usually involve moving to the east or west coast and I'm perfectly happy right here. I think I'll stick to local commercials and mini productions. My work is usually quite pleasurable, although I have had a few problems since we returned from Florida."

"What's happened?" Bree asked, truly interested.

"Well, nothing major. Some minor mix ups, some petty theft, a few things that are really more nuisances than anything else, but they have been distracting and time consuming to clear up. In general I have very few problems with my employees, but it seems that lately someone is out to make my workdays difficult."

Bree knew what that could be like. "I'm sorry, Vic. If there's ever anything I can do to help you…"

"Thanks," he said. "It will work itself out. Things like this always do."

Bree looked at the sky that had now gone completely dark and watched as a full moon made an appearance from her left.

"Do you know what happens now?" she asked Vic with a distinct note of excitement in her voice.

"I'm familiar with night if that's what you mean."

Bree laughed at that as she shook her head at him, "For someone who wants to make his home in the mountains you have apparently missed one of their most beautiful displays." Bree could tell by the look on Vic's face he had no idea where this conversation was going. "It can only happen when the moon is full and the night sky is this clear. Even then it doesn't happen very often."

Vic's curiosity was peaked. "I don't…"

Bree silenced him with a gentle finger on his lips and turned his head to face the moon.

"It won't be long now," she told him.

"Bree, what?"

"Shhh…wait for it."

Vic couldn't argue with the excitement in her voice, so he tried to wait patiently for whatever was coming next. Suddenly, Bree grabbed his hand and he glanced at her in wonder, but she was totally engrossed in the sky.

"Look. Blue sky at night!"

Vic followed her gaze. "Bree this is amazing. Why have I never seen this before now?"

Bree didn't feel the question needed an answer. Not knowing Vic's past, she didn't have one anyway.

Now that the sun was gone and the full moon had risen further in the sky, instead of black they were looking at a beautiful royal blue sky. The moon outlined the tops of the mountains and fingers of mist rested below.

Vic thought it was the most remarkable thing he had ever seen, other than the woman in his arms. He felt Bree's grip on his hand tighten and reached around her shoulders to bring her closer. He was surprised when she easily followed his tug to lean back against him.

Neither spoke as they watched the phenomenon. It lasted only a few more minutes until the moon rose higher. The sky returned to its usual shade of midnight blue and finally to black.

Bree caught her breath, almost as though she had forgotten to breathe while she watched the phenomenon.

Vic leaned around to gaze at her beauty. He didn't know what miracle had dropped this angel in his lap. He wasn't going to question it because he really didn't care, as long as she stayed.

Bree interrupted his train of thought. "This was one of my and Grant's favorite things to see. Doesn't God do amazing artwork?"

"You sure do think a lot about Gra...God." Vic changed his tone and choice of words so as not to pick a fight.

"That's true. At least, I have begun to again lately. Don't you?" Bree asked.

"I don't think so...at least not until recently. My mind does seem to stray in His direction since I met you."

"Are you a believer, Vic?

"In what?" He didn't seem to understand her question.

"In God's promise of Jesus as our Savior. In eternal life through Him. Do you have that personal relationship with Him?"

Vic didn't answer, but instead, rose to spread the blankets out in front of the fire for a makeshift bed. He had found a couple of painter's cloths and placed those down before putting the blankets on top. He appeared to be taking more time with the project than was needed. She could tell by his frown that the subject of God and Jesus had sent Vic into deep thought; thoughts he apparently didn't want to disclose at the moment.

Bree decided to let it go and instead watched Vic's movements quietly as she wondered how she was going to handle this new challenge. With only the two blankets it was obvious Vic thought they were going to share them. How could she possibly lie next to him all night and keep her vow to behave?

Once the bed was made to his satisfaction, Vic came to her, grasped her arm, and pulled her up and over to their newly-made sleeping quarters. Seeing the look on her face, he must have felt the need to explain himself.

"Bree, I'm not a school boy, although I do have to admit to feeling that way when I'm around you. But I always keep my promises, and I will promise you a night of unmolestation."

"That doesn't exist."

"What?"

"Unmolestation…I don't think that word exists."

"Bree, must you always be so difficult?"

"No. Only when you try so hard to be a gentleman. I guess I do have a mean streak after all. I'm not really worried, Vic," she lied. "We are adults and should be able to control our emotions for a few hours."

Vic nodded in agreement as he put more wood on the already blazing fire. "Hopefully this will last through the night. The morning will still be cold until the sun helps bring in heat."

He sat down on the blanket and gently drew her close. He stretched out and pulled her toward him, turning her until her back was to his front, getting her as close to him as possible before he pulled the other blanket around them.

"Vic, I don't think…"

"Shhh…don't think. We have to stay warm, and your clothes won't do that for you, so I'm happy to help. Now be still and try to get some rest. There's somewhere I have decided to take you tomorrow, and you'll need to be well rested for the trip."

"Hmmm…more surprises. I'll try, but I doubt I'll be able to get any rest."

She was asleep almost instantly and slept better in Vic's arms on a hard, cold, wood floor than she had for years alone in the bed she had once shared with Grant.

## Chapter Eleven

Bree awakened to bright sunlight at her back and a brick wall against her face. The wall was covered with cloth and seemed to be breathing. When she realized the wall was Vic's chest, Bree almost laughed out loud. She managed to keep quiet hoping to study Vic for a moment while he was still asleep.

The sun coming in behind her was hitting Vic directly in the face and revealed more scars than she had first noticed. Now that she had the uninterrupted time to really look closely, she could see that they covered most of his face as though he had had extensive surgery. Though she could see the scars well in this light, she knew they weren't noticeable to most people unless they got this close. She felt a pang at that as she discovered she didn't like the thought of anyone being this close to Vic if it wasn't her.

She brought her hands up to touch his face as she wondered at the pain he must have endured to have needed surgery like this. She brushed her fingers over his cheek as her eyes traveled up to his. She was startled to find him looking at her as intently as she was studying him.

"Mornin' Little Lady. Been waiting long?"

"For what?" Bree asked, her voice sounding hoarse to her own ears as she reveled in the endearment rather than taking her usual offense.

"For freedom. It would be difficult for you to move with that block of meat over you."

Bree realized he meant his leg. She had been so caught up in studying his face she hadn't even noticed that she was securely pinned by Vic's left leg. Or was it that she didn't mind? Vic was still mumbling something, but Bree was no longer listening. She had developed an overwhelming urge to kiss him and was wondering how to go about it. Sensing her mood, Vic took the decision out of her hands.

He first kissed her forehead as she had his in their ritual from the night before. He moved down her cheek to her chin, placing tiny kisses on each inch of her face as he went. But he was moving much too slowly to suit Bree. When he reached her chin, Bree took the initiative and placed her mouth in his path.

Vic groaned aloud and began a sensuous assault on her lips. His hands were busy also. Bree hardly felt his shirt move as Vic slid it down her arm so he could place kisses on her shoulder. He moved his mouth to her neck and was aiming lower when suddenly he stopped and pulled the shirt back up. He reached around her to pull the blanket up over her back and pushed away from her until they were no longer touching.

Now what? Surely she hadn't said Grant's name again. It wasn't possible she could be that thoughtless twice in a twenty-four hour period. Bree looked up at Vic's eyes, but he was looking behind her toward the front door. It wasn't until then she heard the voices.

"Seems we're destined to be interrupted, Little Lady," Vic said as two men burst through the front door, laughing as though they had heard the best joke ever. They stopped dead in their tracks when they saw Vic wasn't alone.

"Oops...sorry, Boss," the youngest looking of the two said. "We didn't expect you to have company, especially with the road out. We have a crew on the way to start taking care of that but it will take some time to repair, so, you can take your time." This was said with a knowing smirk. "We'll back on out and you can let us know when it's safe."

"Not necessary, boys," Vic told them.

Oh, really, Bree thought. She was sure her face was flaming, and she was also pretty sure what she would be doing right now if the Lord hadn't seen fit to send the two men in when He did.

"We were just leaving," Vic told them. "Give us a few minutes to get our gear together and we'll be out of your way. Bree, meet Jack and Paul."

Bree peeked out from under the blanket to nod to the two men.

"Nice to meet you, ma'am," they said, as they backed out the door, closing it behind them.

"I'm sorry, Bree. I thought they would probably work today, but I didn't expect them this early on a Sunday. Would you mind gathering up our gear while I go talk to them about the gate and the road?"

Vic jumped up and headed for the door without waiting for her response. Bree was grateful for a few moments alone to regain her composure. By the time Vic returned, she had everything packed and ready to go and had once again asked the Lord for forgiveness for her behavior. She had to wonder why she was so drawn to Vic physically when she hadn't met any other men since Grant who could even make her heart flutter.

The two men were waiting on the porch. Bree saw them wink knowingly at Vic as they passed. Instead of grinning back, Vic looked as though he wanted to punch them.

"It's okay, Vic. We know nothing happened last night," Bree whispered. "Let it go. You have another surprise for me, remember?"

Vic reluctantly let her lead him away, brightening at that reminder. As they hiked back down the mountain, he told her about his surprise.

"Your family?" Bree asked, taken aback by what he had revealed.

"Yes. Did you think the big bad wolf was hatched? They live in the Cove, and I've decided they need to meet you.

Besides, I'm in need of sustenance and no one makes a southern breakfast like Ma. They won't be expecting me today, but they won't mind. So get a move on. I'm starving just thinking about her biscuits."

Back in the SUV, Vic backed down to the gate once again and off the dirt road. The two kept their thoughts about the night before and where the morning was taking them to themselves. If Vic regretted anything that had happened, Bree certainly couldn't tell it. He was focused on driving, but when Bree glanced his way, the hint of a smile told her he was in a good mood. He took back roads Bree hadn't even known existed and soon had them arriving in Cades Cove.

"Vic, I didn't think anyone was allowed to live here anymore. Doesn't the National Park own all of this land now? I've been all over this area and I've never seen any place that looked inhabitable. Most cabins are too old and run down, and the ones that aren't, are open to the public."

"You really have to know what you're looking for to find the place and it's well off any main road. The National Park does own all of the land, but they contract it out and have allowed a few families to stay on to farm and care for the land and animals if their ancestors once lived here. Ma and Pa are the last of their family, so when they are gone no one else can live on that land."

"Wait, Vic…you mean you were raised in the Cove? And what do you mean they are the last? What about you?"

Bree saw the blinds come down. She wondered if Vic even realized he had drawn them.

"Not exactly. I was away from here a lot when I was young. I'll explain it to you some day."

Bree knew she would get no further, and Vic was parking the car anyway. He jumped out to come around and get her. He opened the door and quickly pulled her out and up against his body. Her feet weren't touching the ground, which was just as well, for when Vic held her close Bree could hardly breathe; and no way would her legs stay solid.

Vic wasted no time in claiming her lips. She was expertly kissed then set back on her feet before she could return the favor.

"There, woman. That should keep you satisfied so you don't attack me in front of my family."

"Why you egotistical..." Bree started in, but Vic silenced her with another kiss.

"Behave!" he commanded. "We're in the mountains now where man is beast and woman keeps her place. So start walking and follow me. The rest is on foot."

Before Bree could comment on his bullish behavior, Vic was heading down a hidden path and Bree had to practically run to keep up. He was most definitely in a good mood now, and as the morning warmed, Bree decided to enjoy their hike and call him on his words later.

The trail was long but easy. Bree tried to watch their twists and turns but finally gave up and enjoyed the beautiful fall day.

They rounded a bend and suddenly, looming before them was a log cabin; only this one was nothing like Vic's. This cabin looked like it could be hundreds of years old. As Vic led her onto the porch, Bree could smell that special scent that only the mountains can produce. A blend of hickory smoke, old wood and fresh air, one of her favorite scents. And the heavenly smell of home cooking. She realized she was starving. Vic was watching her intently as they heard footsteps approach from inside and the front door was flung open.

"Vic! We didn't think you'd make it this week when ye weren't here yesterday."

Bree watched in amazement as Vic was embraced by an old woman with a wooden spoon covered in what appeared to be gravy still in her hand. She didn't seem at all intimidated by his size. She was rounded in most places but only slightly taller than Bree herself.

Vic returned the hug and added a kiss on the woman's wrinkled cheek. "Good to see you too, Ma. This is Bree." He pulled Bree around in front of him where she could be viewed more easily.

"Well, hi, Bree." Ma reached out and gave her a hug only slightly less enthusiastic than the one she had given Vic. "Pa, git out here. We got company."

Ma motioned them inside where Bree was transported in thought to the eighteenth century. She didn't think anything in the cabin could be less than a hundred years old; except for maybe Ma, and she might even be close. Bree heard grunting and mumbling as an elderly, though spry man came from the back of the cabin.

"I'm tryin' to git my mornin' nap in. Cain't you let me be for a little while?" His face lit up when he saw Vic, then changed to a look of surprise when he noticed Bree.

"Quit yer gripin', Pa." Ma pointed her spoon toward Bree. "Vic's brought this purdy young thing to visit, and since the mornin' ain't half done I think yer nap can wait."

Pa shook Vic's hand, pulled him in for a hug, turned to Bree, and grabbed her chin in a surprisingly strong grip. He turned her face this way and that before proclaiming, "She'll do. When ye gettin' married?"

"Now Pa, don't start on the young'uns," Ma said. "They just got here. Are y'all hungry?"

"You bet. Are we too late for breakfast?" Vic asked.

"Naw. We went to early church today, so we only had a snack before and ain't been home long. Plop down and I'll finish in the kitchen right quick."

"I can help." Bree started after Ma.

"No, Bree, stay here. Ma works better alone." Bree could tell by his tone that Vic thought she didn't have a clue about cooking.

"Don't be silly, Vic. It'll be fine. I'm sure your dad would like a few minutes with you, and I can help your mom." She didn't notice the questioning looks sent Vic's way by the older couple as she followed Ma into the kitchen.

Less than thirty minutes later, they were all sitting down to an abundant feast of bacon, sausage, eggs, griddle cakes, grits, fried potatoes, biscuits, gravy, late season homegrown tomatoes, and the best coffee Bree had ever tasted. All prepared on an old cast iron wood stove that Bree had helped stoke with kindling. She looked around the kitchen in curiosity and smiled when she spotted no microwave.

Pa and Vic both looked at her with new respect when they found out she had also done more than her share of the cooking.

"Yep, Vic, she'll do awright." Pa grinned a toothless grin, pounded Vic on the back and started into his third helping.

Bree wondered how such a small man could put away so much food.

The next few hours were spent listening as Ma and Pa recounted stories from their youth and their lives in the Cove. Bree found herself enjoying the time more than any she had spent in a long while. Even though it had only been Grant and her, they had been a family unit and Bree hadn't realized how much she had missed being surrounded by people who love you.

Wow. Thoughts of people and having them love her. That had come out of nowhere.

She was also enjoying the heat and smell from the fireplace, so much so that her eyes were starting to drift closed. When Vic pulled her onto his lap and began nuzzling her neck, she started to protest but didn't have the energy to deny herself something she wanted anyway. Ma giggled and Pa offered to give the bride away at their wedding.

All too soon the late afternoon shadows began to form.

"We need to go, Bree, or we won't make it out before dark."

Bree found that she really hated to go. She had already become attached to the aging couple in a short time. They seemed to feel the same judging by the hugs she was getting as she stood to go.

"I suppose you're right, Vic. I hate to go, but I have already relaxed more this weekend than I usually do."

Bree asked Ma and Pa if they ever traveled to Knoxville.

"Hardly ever, Hon," Ma told her. "Vic comes ever' week with any supplies we cain't grow ourselves. We don't git out much 'cept fer church and that's only cause we can hitch up the horses to git there. Church is only about a half mile away. We go to the little one in the Cove."

"Ye prob'ly passed it comin' in," Pa added. "It would sure make a purdy spot for a fall weddin.'"

"Oh, Pa, leave 'em alone. We don't git visitors much bein' so far back in the woods and all so Pa fergits his manners. Sometimes it gits a little lonely but we got each other. Maybe someday ye'll have someone o' yer own, too, and you'll see that that's enough."

Ma looked troubled at Bree's sad expression as Vic hustled her out the door. "Come on, gorgeous, we've got to get you home before dark. You know, pumpkins, carriages, and all that."

Bree smiled at Vic's reference to her as a princess. Surprisingly it didn't bother her at all.

"Ye know, Vic, ye could stay the night," Ma was saying. "We can bunk Bree in the extra room and ye could sleep on the couch. It ain't like it'd be the first time ye done that."

"It's supposed t' be a beauty of a day tomorrow," Pa chimed in. "The horses need t' run and I cain't git around like I ust to. Could ye help an old man out, stay the night, and maybe take the horses for a ride tomorrow?"

Vic smiled at Pa's question, "You know, no one in this room believes you have any problem taking care of your own. About the overnight thing, I can't speak for Bree. I don't know what she has on her calendar for tomorrow."

All eyes were suddenly focused on her. Bree didn't like being put on the spot this way. She did, however, think that a leisurely ride on horseback through the changing fall colors would be heavenly, and another day with Vic wouldn't be half bad either.

"I don't have a toothbrush or hairbrush," Bree told them.

"Don't ye worry none about that," Ma told her. "We keep plenty o' extra stuff cause we're so far from any stores. I'm sure we got all you'd need. I even have some old clothes that quit fittin' me years ago. Believe it or not, I was once 'bout your size."

"Can I get phone service here?" Bree asked Vic.

"I doubt it, but Pa has a radio and can get a ranger to make a call for you. Are you actually considering this?" Vic looked astonished that she was giving in again so easily. "You know, this was also not part of my plan." His eyes were practically begging her to believe him.

"Of course I know that, Vic. It would never occur to you that we still haven't had our hike, and that I might show you up on horseback instead."

Bree was grinning, but Vic was shaking his head, "It always has to be a competition with you, doesn't it, Bree?"

Bree thought for a moment before responding. "No, not always. Only with you. If we can get a message to my office I would love to stay. Kathy isn't accustomed to me not showing up and not calling either. It's been a while since I've ridden, and I'm sure there are lots more stories Pa could tell before we have to turn in tonight."

"I'd be tickled pink to talk about myself for as long as anybody'd listen," Pa told them.

The decision was made. Pa radioed a park ranger who promised a phone call to Kathy. Bree spent the remainder of the day until bedtime, which was apparently eight o'clock in this neck of the woods, getting lost in the past while Vic held her in his arms.

When Bree's head began to fall forward, Vic picked her up, carried her to the spare room and gently lowered her to the bed. He kissed her softly, mumbled something she was too sleepy to make out, and gently pulled an old quilt up under her chin before he left the room.

# Chapter Twelve

Sleepy as she was, Bree tossed fitfully throughout the night from excitement of what the next day might hold. She was awake and up almost before Ma. The two of them had started breakfast when the men entered the kitchen.

Bree was amused by the look of surprise on Vic's face at seeing her already awake. Pa sidled up behind Ma and gave her a quick peck on the cheek, causing her to drop the wooden spoon she was using to stir the biscuit dough, which she promptly picked back up and shook at him, smiling all the while.

Bree loved watching this interplay between the two of them and felt a pang of loss that her parents were no longer alive. This made her thoughts shift to Grant again and what they had shared. Vic saw the sadness on her face and picked her up in his strong arms for a good morning hug followed by a swift kiss before she realized what his intentions were. Bree found she didn't mind it as much as she probably should.

He reluctantly released her, seeing Bree's concentration on what Ma was doing.

"I have never stirred, or seen anyone else stir such thin biscuit dough," Bree told Ma. "I have to ask how you're going to make biscuits from that."

Instead of laughing at her as Bree expected, Ma explained her process. "We make Cathead biscuits up here in these mountains. Ain't ye ever had any?"

"I've never even heard of Cathead biscuits, and have never eaten any unless that's what we had yesterday morning."

Bree gave Ma a sidelong glance to see if she was pulling her leg. She had learned last night that these two mountain folk loved a good joke.

Turned out it was no joke. Bree watched and learned so she could make her own.

After a meal consisting of pretty much every southern breakfast food, including Cathead biscuits made by Bree herself, it was time to start their ride.

Vic headed out the back door. "Pa, how about a hand getting the horses ready?"

Pa stood a bit more slowly. "Well I usually git my first nap in after breakfast, but I guess I can make an exception today."

Bree helped Ma with the clean-up. "It's a good thing we're riding," Bree told Ma while patting her stomach. "I'm pretty sure I couldn't hike a trail if I had to."

Once the men were through the back door Bree started clearing the table, wondering if she could probe Vic's mother for some answers.

"So, I guess you both must really miss Vic since he moved to Knoxville? Pa probably misses all the help he once had doing chores and tending to the farm."

"Oh, Vic weren't never much a part o' that," Ma started, as if realizing she'd said something wrong, she changed the subject. "What do you do back in Knoxville, Bree honey?"

Bree was thrown by the sudden change of subject but decided not to pursue her earlier question. Apparently Vic's parents were as secretive as he was. "I have a modeling agency."

"Yer a model? Well ye certainly are purdy enough."

"Thank you. No, I mean I own an agency that employs models. I have for a few years now."

"Well, I'll be. Ye don't mean it, Why, yer way too young t' be ownin' yer own business. What are ye? Nineteen, twenty?" As usual. Bree's looks belied her age.

"Thanks for the compliment, Ma, but I'm twenty eight. How old is Vic?"

Ma wouldn't look her in the eye, and didn't answer, but instead once again changed the subject. "Ye know Bree, I can finish up here. Why don't ye go git ready for yer ride. I'm sure the men have the horses 'bout ready. Ye'll find my old clothes in the dresser and be sure t' take a jacket. There's one in the closet next t' yer bed. Can be kinda cool early mornins' here in the Cove."

Bree wasn't sure why she was being dismissed, but she didn't know the Andrews well enough to press the point. She left Ma in the kitchen and went to the bathroom to wash up, brush her teeth and get ready. She pulled her hair back behind her ears, tied it with a scarf she had found hanging on the back of the door, glanced in the mirror and had to agree with Ma. Without makeup she did look more like she was barely out of her teens, than the professional she claimed to be.

She did find clothes in the bedroom dresser as Ma had said, and they did fit. Unfortunately, Ma hadn't owned pants. All Bree could find were dresses and long skirts. The choice of blouses wasn't much better. Almost everything had lace and was long sleeved. After much searching, Bree finally found one blouse that she thought might get her through the day. It didn't have long sleeves but it buttoned all the way up to her chin and had lace drizzled all down the front. She settled for a skirt made in the old gaucho style and a pair of high top boots. She felt ridiculous and was thinking that if Vic made even one off-kilter remark she'd put him in his place and ride a horse back to Knoxville on her own. Now, that would be something to attract the wrong kind of attention as she headed down a main highway.

Bree was smiling to herself at the picture in her mind as she looked outside at the beautiful day. Her window faced toward the barn. Vic and Pa were saddling the horses and it looked like they were having a pretty heated discussion. Pa seemed to be ranting on about something while pointing at the cabin. Vic shook his head as if he didn't want to talk about whatever was bothering Pa. Soon the horses were saddled and waiting, so Bree finished hurriedly, remembered to grab a jacket as instructed, and hustled back into the kitchen.

Ma was there with a large bagged lunch and a hug, telling her how beautiful she looked and to be careful to watch for bears. Bree laughed, thinking it had been years since she had seen a bear in the Cove, but promised to be watchful.

Vic and his dad stopped their conversation as she approached, making her think they were most likely discussing her. Vic turned to her with a smile, however, and Pa grinned when he saw what she was wearing.

"Ain't seen that getup in a long while. Stopped fittin' my woman years ago. Glad t' see someone come along who can use 'em again. Have fun now, and watch out fer bears."

Pa chuckled as he walked away. and Bree wondered again at all this concern about bears.

Vic was admiring how she looked in her borrowed clothes, making Bree feel very uncomfortable.

"I know I must look hilarious, Vic, but I couldn't keep wearing the same clothes I've had on since Saturday."

Vic was staring at her so intently, Bree was becoming very uncomfortable. "Bree, you are so beautiful you take my breath away. I have never met a woman who could really pull off that look, even when it was stylish, but on you…" Vic paused, seemingly unable to choose the right words.

"Thank you, Vic. I guess I won't have to be riding this horse down Alcoa Highway after all."

Vic was obviously very confused by that statement, but Bree laughed as they mounted the horses and headed out for Rich Mountain Trail.

Neither felt the need to speak for a while, each being so immersed in their own thoughts that conversation didn't seem essential. The day was glorious with fall colors beginning to tinge the trees. They rode single file since the trail was narrow.

When Bree noticed a strange smell, she reined her horse in to ask Vic about it. Vic had been so engrossed in watching Bree as he rode behind her, he would have run his horse into hers if it hadn't stopped on its own.

"Do you smell that?" she asked Vic. "I know what I think it is, but I haven't smelled that scent in so long. I can't believe there would be a bear this close to the cabin."

Vic froze as he sniffed in an attempt to pick up on what she had smelled. "I think you're right, Bree. There is either a bear very close or one has been here recently."

They both sat very still and listened. Bree looked around in every direction, including up, until her sharp vision paid off. A few feet in front of them, high in a pine tree, was a black bear cub. Bree turned toward Vic, held a finger to her lips, and pointed with her other hand toward the bear. Vic followed the direction she was pointing until he, too, spotted the cub.

Black bears, at one time abundant in the Smokies, had become scarcer during the past decade. Only in the last couple of years had they started to reappear, and not always with good results. Many people looked at them as though they were pets and had found out too late that they weren't. Park rangers had found it necessary to put a few of the mammals down after the bears had attacked hikers.

Seeing the baby omnivore was still a thrill for Bree and Vic. They watched in cautious silence for a few more moments as the cub swatted at insects and cleaned his paws, completely ignoring their presence.

The couple realized at about the same time that they should move on. "Where there's a baby bear, a sow won't be far behind." Vic told her.

Bree nodded her agreement, spurred her horse on with Vic again following close behind. Bree was thinking how fortunate they were to have been given two such beautiful days in a row this time of year.

They started the climb up Rich Mountain and had the trail completely to themselves; not really an odd occurrence for a Monday. Most visitors to the Smokies were weekenders, so Mondays and Tuesdays were usually not overly crowded. Still, fall in the Smokies drew millions of folks each year, more than any other national park. This made it more and more difficult to find secluded areas in the park, no matter how far off the beaten path.

The pair continued on until they reached a turn in the trail at about the five-mile mark where trees had been cleared enough to look down on the Cove. Vic reined in, dismounted, tied his horse to a nearby tree, and came to help her down. Bree didn't need any help, but she was beginning to enjoy playing the role.

"We *have* to stop here, Bree. This is Rich Mountain Overlook. I spent quite a bit of time on this trail a few years ago. You'll love this view," Vic was saying as he reached for her. She expected him to hold her longer than he should, but he set her feet on the ground immediately, took her hand, and led her over to the edge where they could look down on the Cove. She chided herself for the disappointment she felt when he didn't kiss her before he let her go. Her disappointment quickly turned to awe.

"Look at that, Bree. Have you ever seen anything more beautiful?"

She took her eyes off Vic to follow his gaze and her breath caught in her throat. The entire west section of Cades Cove was spread before them in all its glory. It was one of the most beautiful sights Bree had ever seen in the Smokies. She was surprised she had never been here with Grant. She was awestruck and unable to express what she was feeling. Vic had no such difficulty.

He turned her toward him and Bree could see the wonder in his eyes as well, but she also saw something else. Something that would have scared her to death less than a month ago if she had seen it in any other man's eyes. It was the same look she had seen in Grant's eyes the first time they met. The beginnings of love.

Vic placed his hands gently on each side of her face as he studied her quietly. He didn't speak, and Bree couldn't utter a word as he slowly brought his lips to hers for a monumental kiss. Time stopped for Bree as she kissed him back and allowed herself to become fully immersed in Vic's touch.

After a moment she had to break away to catch her breath. "Vic, I need you to stop. I can't think when you do that." Her voice came out in a whisper and sounded all breathy.

"Good. I don't want you to think. It only causes us trouble."

Ignoring her plea, Vic brought his lips to hers once again.

This time Vic was the first to break contact, but he didn't move away, content to stare at her as though he was wondering who she was. Pleading with him hadn't worked so Bree tried to lighten the moment with humor.

"I do declare, Mr. Andrews, you surely know how to sweep a girl off her feet," she told him in what she thought was a pretty good southern drawl, while cooling her face with a make believe fan.

Vic refused to allow her to lessen the impact of their kiss. "Bree, I know what I want to say to you, but I don't know how to say it properly. I feel so much when I'm with you. It's as though I've been dead my whole life and I'm coming alive for the first time. I'm not sure if it's love, or even if I understand what love is, but it's a lot more than a casual emotion. Please tell me you feel the same, or that you at least feel something."

Bree couldn't give him the words he wanted to hear, not yet. It was too early in their relationship for her to make any commitments, no matter how slight, and knowing this made her surprisingly sad.

"Vic, could we slow down a little here? We've really just met. I'm not sure if what you're feeling is infatuation, or maybe I remind you of someone you once loved. Didn't you say earlier that I made you remember someone else? Maybe you should try to sort out your feelings when we get back to our everyday

Cyn Taylor

lives. The beauty in these mountains would set anyone's heart to racing."

Bree could tell he wasn't happy with her response, but he chose once again to let her have her way. He helped her back onto her horse, and they rode to the top of Rich Mountain. The trail would have been strenuous to hike, but the horses had little trouble other than the occasional loose rock. They reached the end of the eight-mile trek faster than either of them wanted.

The fire tower hadn't been used for its original purpose in years. They were able to climb to the top for an even more incredible view. Vic pulled her close as they watched the afternoon shadows play across the vast expanse below them; apparently content to hold her. He demanded no more, and Bree told herself she was glad.

They watched the play of light and color through the Cove for a few moments, climbed down, watered the horses from the animal trough provided by the park, and pulled their lunch out of the saddlebags. Vic spread a quilt on the ground as Bree opened the bags Ma had sent. Seeing the contents she immediately started laughing.

"What is it, Bree? Did you forget to pack food?" Vic was back in a humorous mood, and she was glad for that.

Bree tried to explain between laughs.

"Oh there's food all right. Enough for at least ten people. And something more. A handwritten list of dates the church in the Cove is available for bookings."

"Bree…I had nothing to do with this." Vic was trying to explain, but Bree was too happy in the moment to allow this to bother her.

"It's really kind of sweet that Ma already thinks enough of me to want to encourage a wedding between us, don't you agree?"

Vic could only nod at being caught off guard by her response once again. They ate a wonderful lunch in the Andrews' tradition, made certain they packed away all food and trash for the protection of the bears and other hikers, and started back. The day was over much too soon for both of them.

Pa met them at the barn as they rode up and offered to take care of the horses, knowing they needed to get back to Vic's car or they would have to spend another night. Bree and Vic entered the house to find Ma in her usual spot in front of the stove and had to do some fast talking to assure her they couldn't eat another bite.

Bree called Ma's attention to her own stomach. "Can you tell that I've gained at least five pounds since we got here yesterday?"

Vic joined in. "Me, too. I can't believe you would have any food left in the house after what you've served us since we got here."

Ma was still reluctant to let them leave without more food. "It's the mountin' way, hon. I'll jest get a bag together for your trip back. Bree, honey, why don't you jest keep them clothes till next time? I'm sure we'll be seein' ye again soon."

Bree didn't have the energy to argue and packed up what few items she had brought in preparation to start back home. One last hug all around and Bree and Vic were heading back down the path that only Vic could see. He practically had to drag her the last leg of the trip to the car.

The past few days had taken more of a physical and emotional toll on Bree than she realized, and she suddenly felt exhausted. When they got to the car Vic helped Bree buckle in, got into the driver's seat, and pulled her head onto his shoulder. She didn't even think to protest but snuggled into his arms and was asleep before he had even turned the car toward home.

# Chapter Thirteen

Back at the office Tuesday morning Bree couldn't seem to stay focused. She had awakened long past her usual time, arrived later than she liked for work, and accidentally forgot her cell phone in her car. She had been at her desk for over an hour and so far had accomplished nothing.

Her thoughts kept straying back to the goodnight kiss Vic had given her the evening before. It was already dark when they arrived back at her house after the weekend in the Smokies. Vic could sense her nervousness as she scanned the outside of her home. She hadn't told him about the phone call or the feelings of being watched. She wasn't at the stage yet where she completely trusted this man who was still more of a stranger than a friend. He picked up on her nervousness, but Bree was sure he thought her nerves were due to the kisses they had shared over the weekend.

"Any chance we can continue this evening inside?" Bree sensed Vic's reasons for wanting to come in were for more than casual conversation.

"I'd like to invite you in, Vic, but I have to admit, I'm a little afraid of what might happen between us." Bree knew she'd feel much safer if he was there. She wasn't yet ready to admit that she might be falling for him. "It's true you've been a perfect gentleman since we left the mountains, but in all fairness you did have to focus on driving."

When he laughed at her admission, Bree felt she could end the evening on a light note. She had been wrong. When she offered her hand as a gesture of goodnight, Vic had taken both her hands in his and pulled her close. He placed her hands around his neck as though he knew she wouldn't make that move on her own. Once he released her hands, he had placed his on each side of her face with his thumbs resting in front of her ears. This left his fingers free to massage the back of her head. His eyes never left hers as he slowly lowered his head. Bree stood on the tips of her toes to meet him halfway as she closed her eyes. No warning bells went off. She wanted to feel his lips on hers. Instead she felt his mouth as it lightly brushed the lobe of her ear. She heard him inhale deeply as he pressed his lips harder against her neck.

"How can you still smell like this after an entire weekend?"

Bree tried to make light of his comment. "I always carry my lotion in my purse." The feel of Vic's lips on her neck was doing funny things to her stomach. She tried to catch her breath and explain further. His next move caused all coherent thought to fly right off the porch.

He was touching the side of her mouth with his. Edging his body closer, he finally centered his mouth over hers, encouraging her to kiss him back. She did. Once he realized she wasn't going to pull her face away, Vic moved his hands to her waist. Bree's feet left the floor as he pulled her tightly against his chest and continued to kiss her. Bree could hear bells then. She was light-headed. Her body melded with Vic's like butter on bread. So this was what swooning felt like. As the warning bells grew louder, Bree realized it wasn't bells at all. Smoky must have heard them from inside the house and was demanding to be acknowledged with a high pitched meow.

Bree had pushed away from Vic with a quick "goodnight" and made her way inside. She couldn't acknowledge what she was feeling and had been too tired to try to make any more conversation.

Now that the sensations from the kiss had worn off, sort of, and Bree was alone in her office, she found herself again wondering about Vic's intentions. What if the last few days had only been an act? What if in reality Vic was nothing like he had seemed the past couple of weeks? What if the Vic she had met in Florida was the real Vic? What if she ended up driving herself crazy with all these "what ifs?" Her intercom sounded, breaking her train of thought.

"Hey, boss. I know you'd rather sit around and daydream about Vic Andrews, but we still have more male models to interview. You ready?"

Bree could hear in Kathy's voice that she had lost her enthusiasm for the chore much as Bree had. Both knew this was a necessary step for Smoky Beauties, but after the first few days neither one looked forward to seeing more of the same type of man parade through the office day after day. Bree wanted to chastise Kathy for her accusation about Vic, but it was hard to deny the truth when her assistant had hit it right on the head.

"I guess we might as well get moving. Please send in the first one. How many are scheduled for today again?"

"The final ten." Bree could hear the relief in Kathy's voice.

"Okay. As soon as I send one out, you may as well send another one in if they're waiting. You did schedule them back to back, right? Maybe we can get through these a bit faster."

"Let the games begin," Kathy agreed.

When Bree saw the swagger of the first man through her door, she almost called the whole thing off. She had found three models that would fit the bill so far, but she had shoots scheduled within the month that would require a wider range of talent. She'd need to choose at least three more from the ten she was interviewing today. Otherwise she'd have to start her search all over.

The young man who entered plopped his portfolio down on her desk as he dropped into the chair across from her. He started singing his own praises before Bree had a chance to even introduce herself.

"As you can see I have a lot of experience. And my name is Mr. Wright. Get it?"

His voice was nice but he was slouching in the chair like a fifteen year old at a high school desk. He didn't wait for her reply.

"I have often been told that I am so good looking, I take away from the product I'm selling rather than helping to promote it. That's probably true. I am pretty easy on the eyes. But that isn't my fault. I've always looked this great. What is it you think I'll be selling? Probably something that would feature my abs. I've got incredible abs."

His attitude was self-absorbed and uncaring. Bree wanted to end the interview before it had begun. She knew there weren't that many choices left without generating a whole new list of possible models so she held her disapproval in check and forged ahead.

Bree perused his portfolio. "It looks like you have quite a bit of experience. Have you done much work with other models?"

His answers were brief and uninformative. "My portfolio should speak for itself. I can do whatever you ask."

His head shots were well done but not one boasted a smiling face. In most of the shots the model looked disinterested and in many he was downright scowling. Bree knew within minutes he wasn't right for her agency.

"Thank you for coming in, Mr. Wright. You are my first interview for today. I have nine more to go. Once I have met them all I'll send out a call back for a studio shoot. You will hear from my assistant by Friday if we can use your services."

Bree stood to indicate that the interview was over, but the model didn't rise. He did sit up in the chair as he challenged her dismissal.

"What do you mean you'll call me? My agent assured me I pretty much already had this job."

Bree bristled at his attitude but kept her composure.

"I'm not sure how that's possible. I never saw your portfolio until you threw it on my desk, and I never hire on the spot. We have a very strict vetting process and you are only at the beginning of that. Now as I said, you will get a call by the end of the week if we are interested in screening you further."

That brought a smile to his lips. It was a beautiful smile with perfect teeth. Bree thought he should use it more often, but it still didn't make up for his attitude. He finally stood but made no move to leave. Instead he began unbuttoning his shirt.

"What do you think you're doing?" Having only dealt with females before when interviewing for models, Bree wasn't sure if undressing was customary for the males, but she knew it wasn't happening in her office.

"I think you haven't seen 'enough' of me yet. Once you do, you'll know you don't need to look any further."

"And here I was thinking that I had already seen more than enough," Bree told him. "I am asking you to leave. Now."

He paid no attention to her request as he continued removing his shirt. He threw it over the back of the chair. Bree had to agree that he was certainly on point about his abs. He had started unbuttoning his pants and Bree was voicing another request for his exit when there was a knock on her door. Bree wasted no time in answering.

"Come in. Please." She thought it was probably Kathy. She was surprised and more than a little embarrassed when Vic peeked his head around the corner. His smile turned to a scowl when he saw the model with his pants down to his knees.

"Uh, Bree…Ms. Walters. What exactly is going on here?"

Well, this was going to be fun to explain. Mr. Wright apparently had no problem continuing to undress regardless of who was watching. He was down to taking off his boots so the pants could make their way to the floor when Vic strode purposely across the room.

"Sorry to interrupt, Ms. Walters, but something has come up that we need to take care of immediately. It won't wait." Vic turned to the model who had now regained his seat and was down to one boot. "I'm going to need you to leave."

Bree wanted to argue that Vic was not in charge, but in truth she was glad he had chosen that moment to arrive. She was certain she could have used her no-nonsense voice and gotten Mr. Wright to leave. Probably. But it didn't hurt to have a man Vic's size giving the model his walking papers.

She could tell Mr. Wright wanted to argue. But he was smart enough to realize that Vic was not a man you argued with. Especially without all your clothes on. The model casually pulled his pants back up but left them unbuttoned. He threw his shirt across his right shoulder, picked up his boots, and sauntered toward the door barefoot. When he reached the door he turned, stretching his arms over his head to give her a full on view of his abs. Bree had to admit to herself again that they were fabulous, but she was too close to full blown laughter at Mr. Wright's antics to appreciate his six pack.

"I look forward to hearing from you later in the week. Although you'll probably be calling me tomorrow. I'm sure you don't want to risk losing me. As I said earlier, I am Mr. *'Right.'* "

He glanced at Vic, giving him a smile as he moved by, and left the office door open after he passed through. Bree heard Kathy gasp as he made his exit by her. Mr. Wright might be worth a gasp, but he wasn't Smoky Beauties material.

Once he was gone, Bree turned laughing eyes toward Vic. She was surprised to see that he was not at all amused by what he had witnessed. The scowl was back, and Bree somehow knew that scolding would follow right on the heels of that scowl. She wasn't wrong.

"What in the world was going on in here?" Once again Bree was witnessing the Vic from Florida. She didn't like it one bit. She crossed the room to close the door to allow them privacy in their conversation. She had a feeling it was going to be a loud one. Vic didn't even wait until she was back at her desk. Why did she always have to be right when gauging his moods?

"I asked what was going on in here." Vic was loud enough that Bree was sure the pane rattled in the window behind her.

She tried to calm him with her words. "I believe I told you I was planning to finish all the male model interviews today. Mr. Wright was the first of the day. Did you want something in particular? Kathy knew not to disturb me unless I buzzed her."

Bree was trying to avoid the conversation she was sure Vic wanted to have. Apparently evasive tactics only worked with sane people.

"Oh no. You are not changing the subject. We *are* going to talk about this. Why are you having your potential models undress for you? Isn't that a bit unethical?"

Bree was proud of how well she held her temper in check.

"I did not ask him to undress. When I informed him that no decision would be made about hiring today, he must have decided that I needed a bit more persuading. It did not work in his favor."

"Seems to me his 'favor' was a little further along than it should have been before you told him to stop."

Bree could tell Vic was ready for a shouting match, but she refused to comply. "Well first of all, Vic, you have no say whatsoever in how I conduct my business. Having said that, I was about to ask him to leave, again, when you interrupted. Whatever happened after that is on you. It looked to me like he thought you might be interested in what he had to offer as well."

Vic was at a loss for words with that remark. Bree saw an opportunity and took it.

"Now. Why are you here?"

Bree could tell it wasn't easy for him, but Vic chose not to pursue his line of questioning about the compromising position he thought he had found her in.

"I wanted to ask you something."

"Well...there is this marvelous invention called the telephone. You can carry one in your pocket so it is available wherever you are. It has voice and text capabilities. Did you try using that before you drove over here?"

Vic gave her his heart-stopping smile then. It didn't stop her heart, but it sure made it jump around in her chest.

"I have been calling your cell all morning with no result."

This reminded Bree that she had indeed left it charging in her car. She had gone straight to bed and forgotten to put it on charge after Vic had dropped her home the night before. Not a mistake she ever made until this man had come into her life.

Vic moved closer. "To tell the truth, I needed to spend some time with you. I couldn't go another minute without seeing your beautiful eyes sparkle when you smile."

"And yet you come in here saying and doing things that cause me to frown. Bringing me lunch would have been a more direct route to my smile."

He moved to join her behind the desk. Bree turned as he came around until the desk was at her back leaving her no escape as he moved closer. Now how had she let that happen?

Vic reached for her hand and pulled her to him until they were chest to stomach.

Bree could feel her knees melting into her shoes at the close proximity of this man. This was her work place for heaven's sake. She put a hand against his chest as if to push him away. Somehow it had the opposite effect. Vic lowered his head toward hers. He was going to kiss her again, and she was going to be so unprofessional as to let it happen. He was so close Bree could feel her ears buzzing with anticipation. Nope. That was her intercom.

"Bree…Boss. Is everything okay in there? We have another interviewee ready. Can I send him in?"

Vic and Bree both cleared their throats as they reluctantly parted. Vic moved to put the desk between them once again, as if that would help put their emotions aside as well. It didn't.

"Vic. I really do have to get back to work. Did you really want to see me or was there something else?'

"I really did want to see you. But there is something else. UT has a home game this Saturday. I was hoping you might want to go with me. The weather is supposed to be beautiful."

Bree thought it sounded wonderful. She loved Tennessee football, but it had been years since she had taken time to go to a game. "I would love that, Vic."

"It is a night game so you'll need to dress warm. Although I would love to keep you toasty."

The teasing Vic Andrews was back. This was the man Bree was finding it more and more difficult to dismiss, along with her feelings. The intercom sounded once again.

"The model is still waiting and now Cal is here to discuss the merger, Bree," Kathy was saying.

"Thank you, Kathy. Please tell him to come in."

"Which one. Cal or the model?"

"I'm sorry. Please send Cal in." She turned to Vic with a smile.

"I'm glad you're here. You can meet my attorney." Vic suddenly appeared ill-at-ease as Cal entered the room.

He was smiling as he entered, but that quickly changed to a frown when he saw her face. "Bree, are you sick? Is everything okay?"

"I'm fine, Cal. I must look worse than I realized. I had a very tiring weekend, that's all. Let me introduce…"

Vic didn't let her finish.

"I'll get out of your way now, Bree. I'll call you later."

Vic blew past Cal and was out the door so fast Bree had no opportunity to introduce the two. Well, given the course her relationship with Vic was taking, there would probably be an opportunity for that in the future. She turned back to Cal.

"I can only spare a minute, Cal. Do you have the information I asked for?"

Cal looked concerned as he sat down but let her have her way. "Well, for starters, the name of the company is Mountain Sky Productions. But you already knew that. Seems appropriate, huh?"

Bree had to admit that this could be a good sign, if she believed in that sort of thing. Lately she wasn't sure what she believed in. Maybe this merger could be a good thing for her after all. Cal certainly seemed convinced it would be.

"What about the owner? When can I meet him?"

Cal was hesitant. "Well, that's proving to be a little more difficult than I anticipated. Seems this guy is some sort of recluse. His secretary has been very evasive and won't even give me an appointment date or time. When I spoke with her this morning, she told me to try back next week."

"Well that's certainly odd behavior for someone who has been trying for weeks to get my attention. Aside from that, Cal, I think you have managed to convince me. If you can get this meeting set up, and I feel comfortable with the owner and the company, I'll most likely enter into this merger."

Cal leaped up excitedly and gave Bree a hug before heading for the door.

"Bree, that's great! I'll be with you every step of this process, and I'll see that you never regret this move. I really believe this will help you with your workload and give you more free time. I'll be back in touch as soon as I have a meeting set with Mr. Andrews. Once I tell his secretary about your decision, I'm sure he'll want a meeting ASAP."

Bree nearly dropped in her tracks. "What did you say, Cal?"

"I said I'll get a meeting set up ASAP with Mr. Andrews. I'm sure he'll want to meet soon now that…Bree, what is it? You've gone pale as a ghost!"

Bree was feeling hot and cold all at once and was unable to answer Cal immediately. Her head began to pound and she felt as if she was sinking into the floor. Cal rushed to her side while calling for Kathy, "Bree, what's wrong? Are you ill? What can I do?"

Kathy rushed in and flew to Bree's side.

"What did you do to her?" she asked Cal accusingly while fanning Bree with her hands.

"Nothing, we were just talking."

"First name…what is it?" Bree was trying to ask, but her voice was high and squeaky, and Cal didn't understand her.

"What, Bree? What are you saying?"

"Andrews…what is his first name?"

"It's Victor, Bree, but I'm sure I must have mentioned that before."

"No, Cal, no you didn't mention that…ever. Believe me, I would have remembered."

Cal was looking mystified, but the light was beginning to dawn for Kathy. Bree wasn't paying attention to either of them.

This could not be happening. After all these years she had finally allowed another man to get close to her and now it turned out he was using her to gain access to her company. And she was beginning to think she was in love. How could someone sink this low? He had been trying to trick her from the moment he first knew who she was.

There was no way Vic could be innocent in this. He owned Mountain Sky Productions, and he knew she owned Smoky Beauties. Maybe there was a good explanation, her heart cried. Of course. And maybe the sun would rise in the west tomorrow. No, Vic had been using her…getting her to trust him so that when he finally told her it was he who wanted a business merger, she'd be more than willing. Maybe he was planning to spring it on her when he had softened her up enough to get her into his bed. "Here, darling, let me help you out of all those clothes…and oh, by the way, have you signed those merger papers yet?"

Bree's face flamed at the thought of how close she had come to losing her heart, and more, to this man. Who knew what might have happened if she hadn't called Vic by Grant's name or the construction workers hadn't interrupted them at Vic's house? Bree was busy cursing herself for the fool she had been when Cal's voice finally broke through her thoughts.

"Bree, please…what's going on?"

Bree had forgotten about Cal and Kathy and looked up to see their worried frowns.

"I'm so sorry, guys. Cal, I know you've put a lot of time and effort into this, but I can't do it."

"Can't do what, Bree?"

"I can't let that man into my company. You see, I have met him…have actually spent time with him…and he never once mentioned this. I'm pretty sure I know exactly how things would go once we merged our companies. He'd start out small, little by little he'd manage to get more control until I'd be left with no say about anything. No, Cal, forget the meeting, forget the merger. There is no way I'm going to let this happen."

"But, Bree…"

She was no longer in a mood to listen. "No, Cal!"

Cal stopped immediately. Never in all their years of friendship had Bree raised her voice toward him. Cal looked devastated by her response, but Bree was too distraught herself to notice. Still concerned, Cal gave Bree a business card so she could reach him later that evening if she needed to talk.

"I got a new business cell phone today and a new business number. Let me have your phone and I'll go ahead and save my number for you."

"I don't have my phone. I was charging it in the car this morning and forgot to bring it in."

"Fine. Just keep up with this card until you get the number saved in your phone," he instructed. "My personal number didn't change. Call me on either one if you need anything."

Cal gave her a quick hug and reluctantly made his exit. Kathy followed once she made sure Bree didn't need her help. Bree barely looked up as they left.

When her office door was closed behind them, Bree felt the first teardrop as it fell to her cheek. She took a deep breath and refused to allow the second to fall. Thank goodness she had found out the type of man Vic was before…she refused to think along those lines. Her private line rang and she saw Vic's number scroll across the screen. She wondered how he had gotten that number. No way was she going to talk to him right now. She still had her company and her pride, and she planned to end her relationship with Vic immediately. How dare he try to manipulate her in this way.

"What?" Bree nearly screamed when the intercom beeped.

Kathy apologized timidly for the interruption. "Glory is here for your lunch appointment and the model is still waiting. And Vic is on the phone again. He said you weren't answering your private line. After what just happened, I wasn't sure if I should put him through."

"Thank you, Kathy. I'm sorry I yelled at you. You're right. I'm really not ready to speak to Vic. Would you please cancel the rest of my appointments and send Glory on in? Maybe she can cheer me up."

Bree made a quick trip to her lounge to repair her face. Her mirror reflected stubborn determination, not the tear-streaked image she expected after sustaining such a shock. She had made it through worse. As soon as she dealt personally with Vic Andrews, she would be able to move on and put him out of her life and her mind. Her heart might be a different story.

Glory was waiting in her office when Bree reentered and was her usual bubbly self. The model was so full of life that Bree couldn't help but smile. It still hurt her heart to think how close they had come to losing Glory, and that could also be traced back to Vic, if she stretched it just a little.

"It's so good to see you, Glory. We've hardly had an opportunity to speak since Florida. Do you have a session this afternoon?"

"No, I'm finished for the day. Why?"

"Come on, let's spend the afternoon shopping. I need to get away for a while and we can catch up. Do you have any plans?"

"No, and shopping sounds great. But can we please eat first? I'm starving."

Bree never ceased to be amazed at how much Glory could eat and stay so slim. She was certain no food would stay on her own stomach, but she agreed to lunch as they left her office.

When they got to the garage, Bree had the feeling again of being watched. Glory picked up on her nervousness.

"What is it, Bree?"

Bree tried to shrug it off.

"Oh, I'm sure it's nothing, Glory. I keep having these feelings of being watched, and sometimes followed, since we got back from Florida. I'm sure it's only the stress I've been under for the past few weeks."

"Oh, that reminds me, Bree. I haven't really had a chance to thank you for what you did for me in Florida. I doubt if I made much sense in the hospital down there. I still get the shakes when I think about what could have happened if you and Vic hadn't been there. God was certainly watching over me that day, like He always does. I was stupid for letting myself be coerced into that situation, but Vic helped me to see that it was mostly Brannon's fault and that I should be more careful in the future about letting my vanity get in the way of good choices. So, anyway, thank you."

Glory gave her a hug.

"You're welcome, Glory, but when do you see Vic?" Now why should she care?

"Oh, I'm in contact with Vic a lot. He had lunch at my parents our first Sunday back and usually shares game night with us on Fridays. He still checks on me almost every day either in person or by phone."

Bree felt a new emotion emerging but refused to believe she could be jealous now. Hadn't she convinced herself that Vic was a creep and she should end their relationship as soon as she could?

"So you and Vic are close?"

"Of course," Glory told her, "Everyone in my family loves him, and he's like a brother to me. I would have liked to take our relationship to a different level, but he told me a few days ago that there is a special lady in his life, and he wasn't interested in a romantic connection with anyone but her. He was a gentleman about it. He wouldn't tell me who this special lady is, but she must be someone wonderful to be able to keep his interest. He is an absolutely amazing man."

Glory was so engrossed in her description of Vic that Bree wondered if the girl was going to swoon. Yeah, he was a wonderful man...with a special interest in a certain lady's company. Of course, Vic wouldn't tell Glory his plans. She might let slip to Bree what he was really up to. He probably didn't want anyone to know too soon, not until he had succeeded with his plan to have Bree totally in his pocket so she would sign the merger agreement. Then he could drop her and take up with Glory. Obviously that's who he would prefer to be with regardless of what he had told Glory, considering he had spent more time with her than with Bree in the last few weeks. To her shame, she had to admit that his plan had almost worked.

"....fired Brannon."

"What did you say, Glory?" Glory had been talking the whole time, but Bree had been in her own world of misery and had only caught the last couple of words.

"I said I was glad Vic fired Brannon. He wasn't a very good person. You know, he called me while I was still in the hospital to tell me everything that happened was all my fault. I think Vic fired him before we ever left Florida, and Brannon raised quite a stink over it. Told Vic he'd be sorry for treating him that way and that he'd get even. I don't think Vic wanted to hire him in the first place, but his secretary begged him to. I think Brannon is her cousin or something, and he couldn't find a job because he'd been in prison. I guess that good deed backfired, huh? Vic is such a wonderful person. No wonder the Andrews were willing to help him like he was their own."

"What was that, Glory?" How many more tidbits was Glory going to impart in one conversation?

"What? You mean the Andrews? Vic says they're like a mother and father to him. I don't think they're even related, but they must love him a lot. I think they're the reason Vic had the finances to start his own company. I haven't met them, but if they are anything like Vic, they must be wonderful people too."

"So you keep telling me." Bree was reeling now from information overload. "Glory, I am sorry, but I forgot that I had some papers that needed reviewing, and they have to go out first thing in the morning. Do you mind if we postpone our excursion to another day?"

"Of course not, Bree. You do look a little peaked, too. You should get your work finished and go home and rest. You work way too hard. Maybe we could get together later in the week?"

Bree thought she nodded "Yes" as Glory walked back with her to the garage elevators where they parted company, agreeing to try for dinner later in the week.

"Vic has called three times in the ten minutes since you left. Shall I get him for you?" Kathy asked, surprised to see Bree return so quickly. Bree didn't know what she was going to say or how she intended to handle his deception yet.

"No, thank you. I came back because I realized I have way too much work to do to spend the afternoon idling away my time. Why don't you leave as soon as you have your work caught up? I will probably stay pretty late tonight."

Bree entered her office, locking the door behind her to deter any interruptions. She attempted to work, but with Vic calling every ten to fifteen minutes it proved difficult.

After repeated attempts to concentrate, Bree told Kathy to turn the phones to the service and go home.

Surprisingly, Bree began to have some success with her backlog of work once the phone wasn't ringing and making her think of Vic. Night had fallen before she felt she had accomplished enough that she could go home feeling good about her work day.

Bree finally gathered her things to head home and was somewhat surprised to find that as far as she could tell, she was the only one left in her building.

Bree entered the garage cautiously, once again overcome with the feeling of being watched. Only one other vehicle remained in the garage at this late hour. Bree approached her own car as quickly as she could, reaching for her keys as she walked.

She was unlocking her door when she saw a reflection of movement in her window. Bree turned quickly, thinking she could use her keys as a weapon, but she was too slow. A large figure dressed in black and wearing a ski mask grabbed her purse and pushed Bree against her car. Bree was unable to catch her balance and fell hard to the concrete floor, hitting her head on the car as she went down.

# Chapter Fourteen

Bree was struggling to climb out of a dark well, but the walls were high and slimy. Every time she thought she had a good foothold, she lost it only to fall back to the bottom again. Suddenly there was another person in the well with her and then another. They were whispering to each other, and Bree strained to hear what they were saying. One of them had brought a flashlight and was shining it into her eyes. Bree tried to knock it away because the light made the pounding in her head worse.

"Looks like she's finally coming around," an unfamiliar voice was saying.

"Good," said the voice belonging to the light. "She was out much longer than we expected. That could mean more than just a concussion. I'll get Dr. Massey. He asked to be told as soon as she was awake."

Bree was still attempting to open her eyes a few moments later when she sensed a new presence next to her.

"Has she opened her eyes or said anything yet?" The new voice sounded gentle and very masculine.

"No, Doctor. I came to get you as soon as she started trying to move."

Bree felt a soft touch on her cheek, and the new voice said, "You may as well open your eyes. I'm not going away until I'm certain you're awake."

Cyn Taylor

Bree tried once more to pry her eyelids open, thinking she could be more successful if the flashlight would go away. She slowly opened her eyes to a world filled with dancing lights, colors, and shapes that moved side to side and up and down. Had someone slipped her one of those hallucinogenic drugs she had heard about? The dancing images made her feel nauseous and dizzy, so she closed her eyes again, causing the new voice to chastise her.

"Now, now, none of that. The sooner you can keep your eyes open, the sooner the dizziness and nausea will go away." How did he know she was dizzy and nauseous? Was he the one who had given her the unwanted drug?

"Come on. Try again. Try to focus on one thing. Me, for instance."

Bree did as she was instructed but opened one eye only, trying to focus on the spot where the nice voice was coming from. The voice was right. This time was much better with fewer dancing lights and almost no moving colors. She opened her other eye to find her sight was gradually clearing. She could now see that the new voice belonged to a very pleasant looking young man in a white coat. As she focused on him, his image stopped dancing and stood in one place, smiling down at her.

"Well, hello. I'm Dr. Massey." Of course he was. It said so on the badge pinned to his coat. "Can you tell me who you are?"

What a silly question. Of course she could do that, and she didn't need a badge to help her. But when she tried to answer, she found that her brain and her mouth weren't quite functioning together. She glanced at her own chest to see if maybe there was a badge there too. At her alarmed look, Dr. Massey quieted her thoughts with a gentle touch on her arm.

"Don't panic. What you're experiencing is completely normal after a concussion. Now, very slowly, try again. Tell me your name."

"I'm...I'm... Brianna...Brianna Walters. That's right, isn't it?"

*120*

"So I hear from the man who has been desperately trying to see you for the last few hours. Now, how many of me do you see?"

"Hours?" Bree asked, not answering his question immediately. "I've been here for hours? And I only see one of you. Did you say concussion?"

"Yes. You didn't wake up as soon as I expected, so I want to run a few more tests just to be sure you have no hidden injuries. What is the last thing you remember?"

Bree tried to think back to the last thing that happened before being in the well.

"The well, wait, no…it wasn't a well. I was in…the parking garage…" Bree caught her breath as everything rushed back to her. "The man in the mask! Have you seen him?"

"No, Ms. Walters. No one else was around when the night security guard found you. But don't worry. No one can hurt you here. Do you remember anything else?"

"The man in the garage…he was very tall…and big…and he took my purse…but I don't think he hit me. So why does my head hurt?"

"No, I don't think he hit you either. I think he may have pushed you and you hit your head on your car as you went down or on the concrete once you fell. You'll probably have some nice bruises on your body from landing on the concrete, and a pretty good bruise next to your eye, but with a little rest, I think you'll be okay in a couple of days. I'll go get those tests scheduled. And I think I'd better let your gentleman friend in before he breaks down this door."

As the doctor started for the door, it hit Bree what he was saying.

Her heart gave a leap, and she wanted to tell him not to let anyone in yet. How could Vic have known she was here? Unless…could he have been the one she sensed watching her, and could he have attacked her in the garage? She couldn't see him now. Not while she felt so out of control and vulnerable.

"Doctor, wait, please!" she cried. But it was already too late. A man rushed in as soon as the doctor opened the door. Bree smiled with relief, and only slight disappointment, when she saw it was Cal. She reached up to hug him.

"Well, you certainly seem happier to have me around than you did during our meeting yesterday." Cal grinned, relieved to see she was all right.

"Cal, how did you know I was here? Did you say yesterday? I've been here all night?"

"All night and most of today. The security guard found my business card in your pocket. You must have put the card I gave you there before you left your office. It's a good thing you did, because the guard didn't know who else to call. I've been waiting to make sure you were okay. Annie went home to be with the kids when it got so late last night. I told her I'd stay and get you home. I called Kathy this morning to let her know you would be unavailable today. I didn't tell her what happened. You've seemed so distraught lately; I wasn't sure how much information you'd want her to have."

"Oh, Cal, I'm so sorry for the way I spoke to you." Bree felt the tears start again and this time she was unable to stop them. This was a side of her character Bree had kept hidden since Grant's death. She could tell Cal didn't quite know how to handle it.

"Hey, don't cry," Cal said. "I wasn't mad, and I know you'll tell me your reasons when you're ready. Please don't worry about that now. The police have been here off and on since last night, and they're waiting to speak to you now. Do you think you're up to it?"

"I think so," Bree said as she tried to get the tears to stop. "Might as well get this over with. Can you stay?"

"Of course. Annie insisted I stay with you as long as you need me. She's pretty amazing, you know."

"Yes, she is, Cal. You are both lucky to have each other. I miss Grant so much when I see the two of you together."

"It isn't luck, Bree, and you know it. The Lord put us together as He did you and Grant, and He'll bring someone else just as wonderful into your life when and if the time is right."

"Oh, Cal, I wish I had your faith. Mine seems to be slipping further and further away."

"Don't worry, Bree. I believe God is doing a work in your life, and you'll understand it when you're prepared to accept it. Now, I'll go get the police."

Once again Bree was amazed at this loving man who remained her friend no matter what, and who seemed to know and understand her better than she understood herself. Cal stayed with her while she spoke to the officers.

Trying to describe her assailant to the police proved more difficult and tiring than Bree had anticipated. The older of the two officers started the questions. "So, ma'am, tell us again exactly what happened."

Bree wasn't sure she liked being a ma'am. But she knew they were being polite. She tried to recount her every move from the time she left her office. It was difficult with the way her head ached.

"And you're sure you can't give us any more information about your assailant?" The eldest of the two officers was respectful but persistent.

"I'm not sure what you want me to say, officers. I barely caught a glimpse of him before he knocked me down. Mostly as a reflection in my car window. His face was completely covered by a mask and he was dressed in dark clothes. He didn't speak. He seemed tall and broad, but I'm a bit on the short side so it's really hard to be sure of that. I don't know what else I can I tell you."

The younger of the two stole a glance at Cal. Bree wondered what that meant.

"Cal, is there something you aren't telling me?"

Before he could speak, the officer took over the conversation.

"Your attorney told us you were having suspicions of being followed. That you had received a threatening phone call. How long has that been going on?"

Bree gave Cal the best frown she could muster with her headache.

"What ever happened to attorney/client privilege, Cal?"

"Sorry, Bree. That doesn't apply if my client's life is in danger."

"Who says I'm in danger? Whoever attacked me could have injured me more than they did. I was out cold and they apparently chose to leave me alone. How does that put my life in danger?"

"Your attorney is right, ma'am." This from the older officer. "We can't discount any fact. Your feelings of being followed, the phone call, and the attack. That all adds up to be possibly life threatening. We're saying that you need to exercise caution. Don't be alone in the parking garage again, be watchful when you're out at night, keep your doors locked, that sort of thing."

"In other words, live my life in fear?"

"Bree. They're only doing their job here." Cal came to stand by her bed. "You were attacked. It wouldn't hurt to be more cautious for a bit."

Despite wanting to be in control, she nodded in agreement. She had to admit she wasn't feeling so confident when she was alone these days.

"Thank you, gentlemen. I will take your advice to heart and attempt to be more cautious. I'm sorry I can't be more help with a description. Do you think there is any chance you can catch him?"

The officers looked at each other before answering. But Bree already knew what their response would be. The younger officer took the lead. "We're sorry, ma'am. Unless they attempt to use a credit card or an I.D. from your purse, we don't have enough to go on to even start a search. Keep us in the loop if anything else happens. Is there anyone you can think of who would want to harm you? Anyone you've had a disagreement with lately?"

Bree thought of Chris. He had been very angry the last time they had been together. But could he really be the type of person who would do this? She also thought about Vic. It hurt too much to think he could be responsible. In spite of what had happened yesterday. Whoever it was, Bree was going to handle it on her own. She chose to keep her thoughts to herself as the two officers left.

Then it was Cal's turn. "I know you, Bree. I know what you're thinking."

"And what might that be, Cal?"

"You're thinking you can handle this on your own."

Wow. Did he know her or what?

"You're thinking you can go home, pretend this never happened, and everything will be fine. But please, Bree, take this seriously. Promise me that you will be more cautious."

Bree knew Cal had only her best interests at heart, and she was far too exhausted to argue.

"Fine, Cal. I promise. Now go home. I can't leave until the tests are finished so there really is no need for you to stay. I'm sure Annie and the kids think you've abandoned them."

Cal gave her a quick peck on the cheek and did as she asked, promising to return to take her home when she finished the remainder of her tests.

The testing was painless and quick. Bree napped fitfully off and on as she waited for Cal to return. She drifted in and out of sleep, moving through dreams filled with images of large men in black who looked like Vic, then Grant, then Chris, then like the man in the mask who had accosted her the night before. By the time Cal returned to take her home, she looked and felt worse than when he had left; but she was more than ready to leave the hospital.

As the nurse pushed her wheelchair out to Cal's car, Bree asked him to drive her to her office.

"Bree, I don't think that's a good idea at all. It's already after eight and you probably can't get in your office anyway."

"Cal, I have an extra set of keys there and I need those to get in my house. My cell should still be in my car as well. Security can let me in my office, and I want to drive my car home, otherwise someone will have to get me to work tomorrow. Hopefully the man who accosted me didn't steal my car. I really need to do this tonight."

"Now, Bree, the doctor said a couple of days rest…not one night."

"Really, Cal, I'll be fine. You know how I hate to rely on other people."

Cal finally gave in, "Okay, Bree. But I'm going up with you and following you home. All right?"

"Yes, Mother."

"Hey. Don't get smart with me or I'll have to ground you."

As they traveled, Bree talked to Cal about what had been going on in her life recently. She shared the time she had spent with Vic from the very beginning, hoping Cal would understand her reasons for refusing to do business with Mountain Sky Productions. He voiced his agreement with her decision. It was so very good to talk to someone she could trust.

"Cal…I hope you know how much I appreciate all you, and Annie, do for me…how dear you both are to me."

Cal tried to shrug it off, embarrassed by her seriousness. "Aw, shucks, ma'am, twern't nothing."

Bree knew Cal hated to be in the spotlight, but she felt it was important that he know how she truly felt. She had taken him and Annie for granted all the years she had known them and that had to stop. It was time to give something back.

"Cal, I have something I'm trying to work out in my life right now, some of it you already know about, some you don't. Anyway, as soon as I can get a handle on all that's going on… well, I'd really like to spend some time with you and your family again, apart from work. Do you think Annie would be willing?"

Cal's face lit up. "Bree, Annie would be thrilled. She's missed seeing you and has asked me over and over why you don't come around anymore. To be honest, I don't really understand that myself. We were all so close when Grant was alive. We miss him too, you know."

If it was possible, Bree felt even worse hearing Cal's words. She had been so very selfish, closing into herself and refusing to share her grief with her closest friends, or acknowledge theirs.

"Cal, I can't apologize enough. Do you think you and Annie could ever forgive me?"

"Bree, we love you, of course we can forgive you. But you and I both know there is another relationship that's more important, and you need to get that right again so you can start to live the life you're supposed to be living. You know you belong to God, and it grieves Him to see you as you've been since Grant's death. It's time to move on. Don't you agree?"

"Yes, Cal, I do. And I intend to try. I have to figure out how to begin."

Cal was pulling in next to Bree's car. She whispered a quick prayer of thanks that it was still there.

She asked Cal to sit and pray with her before they went up to her office. She prayed for forgiveness for the sins she had committed in the years since she had lost Grant, for her lack of faith that God had only her best interests at heart, and for courage to proceed in the direction He had chosen for her. She realized that she had drifted away so gradually that she had barely even noticed. Thank goodness Cal and Annie hadn't given up and left her in her misery. Thank goodness for a Heavenly Father who never gives up on His children and keeps calling them back no matter how far they stray.

When she finished praying, Bree felt that the load of the last few years was lessened and she could finally move ahead with her life. She knew it wasn't going to be easy, but she also knew that God was back where He belonged in her life, and with His guidance she could face whatever He had planned. She hugged Cal and once again thanked God for sending her such true friends as Cal and Annie.

Cal walked her upstairs where they met the security guard who had been on duty and had helped Bree the night before.

"Ms. Walters. It's so good to see you up and about. I was so worried about you when I found you. My family and I have been praying for you."

He told her his name was Sam. Bree was embarrassed that she had worked in the same building with him for years and had never even spoken to him. He opened her office for her and she was careful to thank him for his timely rounds. He had found her quickly and known exactly what to do.

"Now that I've met you, Sam, I hope we can become friends." Bree said. "I don't know what would have happened to me if you hadn't been here."

Sam was embarrassed by her thanks.

"I did what any good Christian would have done, ma'am."

"Maybe, maybe not." Bree said. "But I am very grateful you were there and willing to do what you did."

Once Bree retrieved her keys, Sam walked to the elevator with them. "I've kind of watched you grow up in this building, ma'am. I'm so glad the Lord chose to spare your life and any serious injury. From now on if you work late, you give me a call and I'll see you safe to your car. No need at all for you to be alone in this building or the garage."

Bree certainly was getting her eyes opened tonight. Was everyone around her a believer and she had been so caught up in her own world she hadn't even noticed?

No, she was sure of at least one person who wasn't. Although, Vic had alluded to God when they were stranded in his house, so maybe she should give him the benefit of the doubt before she made any rash decisions. She certainly hadn't been on her best behavior either since they met. But she still wasn't convinced he could be trusted. Sam left them at the elevator wishing her well and reminding her once again to call him any time.

She and Cal rode the elevator down together. As Bree approached her car, Cal noticed her shudder and tried to reason with her once again. "Bree, why don't I follow you home? It's completely dark now, and I'm sure you didn't leave any lights on when you left for work yesterday morning. You won't find a dark house very welcoming after what you've been through."

"Thank you, Cal but that really isn't necessary. I have to go home alone eventually so…"

"It doesn't have to be tonight, Bree."

"Yes, Cal, I think it does. I think it's time to exercise my reborn faith."

Cal was shaking his head at her stubbornness. "Will you at least call us when you get home?"

"Yes, Cal, I will call. Now will you stop worrying?"

"Okay, okay. Do you want me to take you tomorrow to get a new license and…"

Bree interrupted. "Cal, I'll manage. Thank you. You have your own life, and I've already asked far too much of you. I'll be fine."

"Bree, I don't think you're taking this attack seriously enough. You could have been hurt so much worse."

"Cal, purse snatches happen every day. The only difference here is that it happened to me. We don't really even know if I was a random target or in the wrong place at the wrong time. Now, go home to your family and stop worrying about me. And Cal, thank you, really…for everything. And please thank Annie for me until I can do that myself."

Bree gave him a hug before climbing into her car; her head was really beginning to throb now as the events of the last twenty-four hours were catching up to her. She wanted nothing more than to get home, soak in a nice hot tub and tell Smoky all about recent events.

Poor Smoky. He'd been alone for almost two days and probably thought she'd abandoned him. He would probably ignore her for a few hours until he thought she had been chastised enough for her negligence. Thank goodness her Heavenly Father wasn't as judgmental as her cat.

# Chapter Fifteen

The drive home seemed to take forever. The pounding in Bree's head made her wish she had listened to Cal and allowed him to bring her home. Strangely, when she arrived home, her garage door opener didn't work. She parked in her driveway and entered her house through the back door, once again forgetting her cell phone. Thank goodness she had gone back to her office for the second set of keys.

She flipped the switch on the kitchen wall but nothing happened. She thought she heard Smoky meowing somewhere in the house and called out to him.

"Smoky, where are you? Come here, kitty."

Bree cautiously found her way into the dark hallway and tried the lights there. Still nothing. Thinking that a fuse must have blown, she had started back to her car for her cell phone and a flashlight when she was grabbed from behind. She screamed and began to fight her captor. He was much stronger than she was. He had reached around to put his hand over her mouth to prevent her from calling out again when she was let go so suddenly she fell to the floor.

"Bree, get out of here and call the police!" It was Vic. Where had he come from?

Not stopping to think, she did as he said and ran back to her car. She jumped in and locked the door behind her as she grabbed her cell and dialed 911. As soon as she had given the information to the operator, she carried her phone back into the house to search out Vic and the man who had attacked her. This time she remembered the flashlight as well.

"Vic, where are you?" Bree was shining her flashlight around the kitchen but couldn't see, or hear anything. She heard footsteps and Vic appeared in her light. He grabbed her in a ferocious hug as though he'd never let her go again.

"It's okay, he's gone. Did he hurt you? Are you all right?" Vic wasn't lessening his hold on her, and Bree could feel every bruise that Dr. Massey had predicted.

"Please, Vic, let me go." Vic released her immediately when he heard the pain in her voice.

"Bree, what is it? What did he do?"

"This guy didn't have a chance to do anything. You were here so quickly that I had only just arrived right in front of you." She would ask him later about that coincidence. "Would you mind checking the fuse box? Take the flashlight. The box is in the basement. I need to find Smoky."

Using the light from her cell, Bree started her search. Smoky chose that moment to jump into her arms. Once again her heart did a dangerous pause. The cowardly cat had finally decided to come out so Bree was sure the coast was clear. With Smoky safe, Bree started with Vic to the basement. But he was having none of that.

"No, Bree, you wait here. The stairs will be tricky in the dark, even with a flashlight, and you don't need to add a fall on top of what just happened. This has been a frightening experience, I know, but I'm sure we're the only ones in the house now," Vic assured her as he led her to the couch. "Sit here and I'll be right back."

"No, Vic. I don't want to wait here alone. I want to come with you."

"I said no, Bree. Listen, it's okay. The guy ran out of the house and I think toward the woods when I told you to call the police. I'm sure he won't be back tonight. Now please, sit here while I get the lights back on. I promise I'll be right back."

Bree nodded and realized he couldn't see her, so she replied out loud. "Okay, Vic, but please hurry." He gave her hand a quick squeeze and was gone.

Of course Vic couldn't understand why she was so frightened. He didn't know she'd now been attacked twice in as many days. She heard the sirens at the same time the lights in the kitchen popped on. She reached for a lamp by the couch and turned it on as Vic re-entered the room.

"Goodness, Bree! I thought you said you weren't hurt." Vic was accusing and concerned all at the same time. Bree hadn't looked in a mirror since the first attack and had no idea she was sporting a pretty good black eye from her fall the night before.

Vic pulled her into his arms, and she went willingly. It felt so good to let him hold her. Why did he have to be so deceitful? Why couldn't he have just told her the truth about the merger? He'd had ample opportunity when they were in his cabin but had chosen not to discuss it.

Vic felt her withdrawing but loosened his hold only slightly to ask, "Bree what is it? What's happened? You wouldn't take my calls or return them yesterday, and when I called today, all Kathy would say was that you were unavailable. I felt I had no choice but to come here. I want to know what's going on, and I want to know now."

She let herself rest against him for another moment, and that was how the police found them when they burst in through the front door, guns at ready. Bree moved out of Vic's embrace and was surprised but grateful when she recognized the same officers she had met earlier at the hospital.

"Thank you for coming so quickly, gentlemen. It's good to see you again." Bree was amazed at her own calm. Once Vic had arrived, Bree's fear had subsided. She thought it was too bad her bravery came and went with Vic, since he seemed so undisciplined himself.

The officers were eyeing Vic suspiciously so Bree thought she had better introduce him. "This is Vic Andrews. He's…a friend. Everything's fine now. Mr. Andrews showed up just after I arrived home and scared away a man who was waiting for me inside. We haven't examined the doors or windows, but I'm going to guess this was the same man who attacked me yesterday and he used the keys he stole from me to get in the house. If you'll check, I'll bet you won't find any sign of forced entry." Wow. Still calm and even telling the police how to do their job.

"So you think it may be the same man from last night, but you're pretty sure he's gone now?" The youngest of the two officers asked.

"Mr. Andrews is pretty sure he scared him into the woods behind the house, and he certainly seemed about the same size as the man last night. It's hard to know for certain because the power wasn't working in the house, and I didn't see him. He felt large."

"Well, we'll check around outside, maybe visit a couple of your neighbors, then come back for your statement." The older officer said. "You seem awfully calm considering what you've been through the past couple of days. Are you sure you're all right?"

"I'm doing fine. I'll start a pot of coffee," Bree said, and turned toward the kitchen as they headed out the front door.

No sooner were they out the door than Vic was spinning her around to face him. "Bree, what in the world has happened since I saw you last? What about last night, and why do you know these officers so well? And why are you bruised and in pain? I want some answers and fast!"

Vic was working himself into a fine rage, so Bree recounted for him all that had taken place since she had seen him last. She could tell that her passiveness about such an extreme situation was beginning to worry Vic.

"Bree, why didn't you call me? I'm the one who should have been with you in the hospital. I'm the one who should have brought you home, and I'm definitely the one who's going to take care of you now."

"Oh really, Vic? And why is that? Are you basing these assumptions on your opinion that we have some kind of a relationship going on? Or maybe you're afraid something might happen to me before you've had time to get your hands on my company?" Vic at least had the decency to look a bit ashamed at her last statement.

"Now be honest, Vic. Oh wait. You don't know how to do that, do you? Be honest, I mean. Because if you had wanted to be honest, you would have already told me that you own Mountain Sky Productions, the company that wants to merge with mine. Right?"

Vic had gone completely still and couldn't seem to look her in the eye. "What are you talking about, Bree?"

"It's a little late to play the innocent, Vic. I have a very good friend who also happens to be my attorney. I was about to introduce you to him before you ran out of my office so fast yesterday. Did you think he wouldn't tell me who owned Mountain Sky Productions? Or did you think that maybe I was stupid enough that I would agree to the merger without ever meeting you or asking for your name? And to think I went so far as to ask your opinion about whether or not I should proceed with this merger. It isn't as though you haven't had ample opportunities to tell me. Were you afraid the seduction of the owner hadn't gone far enough yet? Did you want me completely under your control before you told me?"

Vic actually had the nerve to look hurt at her accusations.

"Bree, how can you say that? How can you believe any of what you're thinking? I thought you had gotten to know the real me. I thought we were beginning to mean something to each other."

"Apparently I do know the real you. He's the man I met in Florida, isn't he? That's the real you, isn't it, Vic? The time we've spent together has been play acting for you, hasn't it?

You've been spending time with me until it wasn't necessary anymore and you could take up with Glory."

Vic looked completely shocked at that accusation. "With Glory? What has she got to do with any of this? Bree, I really am confused."

But Bree wasn't listening. "Well, it almost worked, but thankfully I found out in time. Your plan has failed. I still have my company, you can have Glory, and I want you out of my life!" So much for remaining calm.

Bree's voice had raised several decibels until she was almost screaming. The police burst in through the back door with guns in hand once again. They lowered their weapons when they saw only Vic with her.

"Sorry, Ms. Walters. We heard shouting and thought you were in trouble. Are you...in trouble? Are you all right?"

Bree placed her hands on either side of her head. "Would everyone please stop asking me that?" She really was shouting now and knew she needed to get herself under control. "I'm sorry, officers. None of this is your fault...I'm a little on edge still. I'll make your coffee now."

"Bree, you talk to the officers, and I'll make the coffee," Vic said, apparently still thinking he was in control.

Bree tried to regain her calm, "No, thanks, Vic," she said. "You've done quite enough. I'll be fine now, and I think you should go home."

"I'm not leaving here tonight, Bree, so you may as well save your breath. I'll get the coffee. You finish with the police."

Bree was too drained to continue arguing and decided it might be best to allow Vic to think he was in control, for now. She'd deal with him later after she had given a report to the officers.

Vic moved off to the kitchen while Bree told the police all that had taken place once she had arrived home.

"You're probably right that this man tonight is the same one who attacked you last night. Once we've confirmed that there is no sign of forced entry, we'll be pretty sure of that."

Both officers were doing their best to convince her she should spend the night away from her house when Vic returned.

"Ms. Walters, be reasonable. This man has already tried at least twice to hurt you. Isn't there somewhere you can stay for a few days to give us a chance to find out who he is and catch him?"

"Gentlemen, I refuse to be run out of my own home."

"Ms. Walters, please, you have nothing to prove, and you may be in real danger. We can post an officer here for tonight, but it could take some time to find this man. Especially since we don't have a description, and we can't keep someone here indefinitely. Please, for your own safety, stay somewhere else, even if it's for a short while."

"That won't be necessary, gentlemen," Vic interjected. "Ms. Walters will be perfectly safe here...with me. I'm not leaving her alone until this man is found."

Vic handed coffee to the officers and sat down on the couch beside Bree, placing a protective arm around her shoulders. Bree tried to shrug him off, but he pulled her closer. The way Vic was scowling, neither officer looked convinced that she would be any safer with him than with an unknown assailant.

"I am more than capable of caring for Ms. Walters." Vic said. "I'll take the responsibility of seeing that no harm comes to her. If you've finished here, may I suggest that you leave so that she can rest. She has apparently had two extremely straining days and is probably near exhaustion." Bree had to agree with that.

The officers rose to leave as Vic had suggested, but asked to speak to her privately, outside, before they got in their car.

"Ms. Walters, are you going to be okay with this man?" The youngest of the two asked. "He seems...I don't know... angry...maybe at you. Are you sure you'll be all right alone with him?"

They seemed truly concerned, so Bree tried to make light of the situation. "Thank you for caring about my safety, but I don't think Mr. Andrews' anger is directed at me. I can handle him." Sure she could. But she did plan to give him his walking papers as soon as the police were gone.

"Well...if you're sure. But take my card," the older officer said. "And do not hesitate to call me at any time, please."

"Thank you," Bree told them both. "I do appreciate all you've done."

The officers hesitated for another moment and must have decided there was nothing more they could do to convince her to see things their way.

Bree waited until the lights from the cruiser had disappeared over the last hill before heading slowly back into her house. Vic was on the couch with a traitorous cat in his lap. He placed Smoky on the floor, and rose to meet her.

"All right, Bree, let's get this out in the open."

Sure. Now he wanted to talk.

"It's true that I have known you were the owner of the modeling agency I wanted to merge with since the first day I saw you in your office. Before that, I knew that the owner was Brianna Walters. But you know that already.

"At first, I thought I would get to know you a little...see how your mind worked...how you ran your business. But I felt something...unusual for you, almost from the beginning." He ignored her scoff and continued. "Bree, I'm in love with you. I think I have been since the first time I touched you...maybe before that...I don't know. When I'm with you I feel as though we've been together forever. Since I met you I can't focus on business or think of anything but you and the life I know we can have. I couldn't offer you advice on the merger. That would have been unethical. If I had told you that I was the potential partner, it could have influenced your decision and...I thought maybe you were beginning to feel as I was. I couldn't risk spoiling that. I'm certain that a merger of my company and yours would be beneficial for us both, but the decision had to be yours alone. Bree, you have got to believe that I would never deliberately hurt you. And your business is not what I am most interested in about you. As I said...I love you."

Bree knew Vic was yearning for a certain response from her, but she couldn't say what he wanted to hear. Not yet. Maybe not ever. Instead she had a question of her own to ask. "Vic, if I had asked you straight out if you owned Mountain Sky Productions, would you have told me?"

"Of course, Bree. I never set out to deceive you. I wanted our relationship to be one of love and trust."

He sounded so sincere, but how could she open her heart and let him back in? She was still stinging from the hurt of the last two days, and not from the physical pain.

"You know, Vic, I've had difficulty separating my former feelings for Grant from my new feelings for you. Sometimes you seem so much alike to me I would swear I was talking to him, touching him. At other times I see no resemblance at all in your character, and not much in your looks. I'm not sure I've dealt with my past effectively enough to allow you in my present, or my future. Maybe I could learn to trust you if you could open up a little more about your past. If I knew for certain where you've been and how you grew up, maybe I could completely separate you from Grant."

It was amazing. Bree watched in disbelief as the same shutters she had grown accustomed to seeing dropped right back into place. The man who had been so desperate to be a part of her life a minute ago was now completely withdrawing.

"You're probably right, Bree. We've talked enough for tonight. At least tell me you won't shut me completely out of your life yet. Give me time to set things right."

Bree thought of the heartache this man had already caused her in such a short period of time. She was certain the future would hold even more if she allowed him to remain in her life. Still, when he was looking at her as he was now... "All right, Vic. We won't decide anything right this minute. I've been phys-ically and emotionally distraught since yesterday, so now is not a good time to make any decisions about the future. I'm too tired to fight anymore, so if you still want to stay, you can take the extra bedroom. I'm going to bed now." With that, Bree picked up Smoky, leaving Vic to fend for himself, and dragged her tired body into bed. Her mind might not be convinced, but in her heart she knew Vic would never hurt her, not physically anyway.

Exhausted, she fell asleep quickly. Sometime in the middle of the night she awakened suddenly and listened for…what? Smoky was fast asleep on the foot of her bed, and she could hear no noise but that of him snoring. Maybe Vic had gotten up for something.

She rose to check and see if he was still around. True to his word, Vic was in the spare room, sleeping soundly. Some bodyguard he was. Bree approached the bed where moonlight was spilling in through the window and casting shadows across Vic's body.

He had pushed the covers down to his waist, and his hair was falling over his forehead. Relaxed in sleep, he looked so much like Grant that Bree's heart ached. So many similarities, but so different, too. Unwittingly Bree reached out to brush the strand of hair back from his forehead. She let out a gasp as she was grabbed and pulled off the floor. She found herself chest to chest with Vic and only her thin t-shirt between them.

"Little Lady, don't you know not to sneak up on a man when he's sleeping?"

Bree couldn't answer. Her hands were on Vic's chest and the heat from his body was penetrating to her toes. Her desire flared instantly. Other than Grant, she had never wanted a man this much. She still struggled to understand why Vic had such a profound effect on her feelings. And how she could go from cold to hot so quickly with only a brief touch from the man. Vic, however, appeared unaffected by the close proximity and was still talking.

"Don't you think I deserve a kiss for saving your life tonight?"

"My life was hardly in danger." She wasn't really convinced of that.

"So you don't want to kiss me?"

Of course she did. With every fiber of her being. "I didn't say that, but…Vic…let me go…please."

Vic gave her a long, searching look but finally did as she asked. She made her way back to her own bed, closed and locked the door, and spent the remainder of the night tossing back and forth while visions of Vic and Grant wreaked havoc with her thoughts. Just before she dropped into a fitful sleep, she realized what she had to do and where she needed to go for answers.

# Chapter Sixteen

Bree awakened early the next morning. After using makeup to try and repair the damage to her face, she gave up and decided it would have to do. She tiptoed out of the house, keeping her noise to a minimum so that Vic wouldn't wake and question her on where she was going.

His car was parked behind hers in the driveway, but she was able to maneuver around it. What she had to do could only be done alone, without Vic to try and coerce her. She stopped only for coffee before she turned her car toward Cades Cove. She stayed well under the speed limit, knowing it would be hard to explain why she was driving without a license if she was pulled over.

Driving to the Cove seemed to take longer than usual in her exhausted state. Bree drove to where she thought Vic had parked when they had come before. She took the few supplies she had brought along and headed up, what she hoped, was the same trail she had taken with Vic. She had been walking for what felt like hours when the Andrews' cabin finally came into view. She breathed a sigh of relief as she approached the cabin with a determined stride, her mind set on solving the mystery that was Vic Andrews.

When there was no response to her knock, Bree groaned inwardly thinking that if she had come all this way for nothing it would be more than she could take after the week she had experienced. But Vic had said the Andrews rarely left the cabin unless he took them somewhere, and Bree was pretty sure he could not have gotten here before her, even if he could have figured out this was her destination. She knocked again, more insistently, and finally heard the shuffle of feet from inside the cabin.

"I'm comin', I'm comin'...keep yer pants on!" Followed by mumbles of, "a person cain't take a decent nap no more without some varmint sneakin' up and causin' a ruckus." The door opened, and Pa's scowl turned to an all-out grin when he saw Bree.

"Well, don't just stand there, girlie, come in, come in. Good t' see ye. Ain't had so much company in years." Grabbing her arm, he pulled her inside before peering around her. His attention was drawn back to her bruises. "What on earth happened to yer face, girlie? And where's our Vic?"

"He isn't with me today, Pa. I've come alone. I'll explain about the bruises on my face later. I'd like to talk to you and Ma, if that's all right. It's about Vic."

Pa looked alarmed. "Is Vic okay?"

"Don't worry, nothing is wrong. At least he was fine when I last saw him. I have some questions I hope you can answer. Would you mind?"

"Why, we'd love to talk to ye about Vic. He's one of our favorite subjects. Have a seat and I'll go git Ma."

He disappeared through the kitchen door. Bree sat down by the fire in a rocker that had probably been around since the days of Davy Crockett. She could hear raised voices coming from the back of the house. It sounded as though Ma and Pa were arguing. Bree hoped she wasn't the cause. She rose as Ma came through the kitchen door and was greeted with a big hug and a kiss on the cheek.

"It sure is good to see ye, Bree girl." Ma said. "Gits kinda lonely up here with no one but this old bear t' talk to. I'm awful curious about those bruises, but Pa said ye had somethin' important ta say. Now set back down and I'll git you some biscuits and jam and a good strong cup o'hot tea. We always take a tea break durin' the day since Vic took a likin' to it, and ye sure look like ye could use it,"

Bree started to object, but she knew there would be no serious conversation until Ma made sure her guest had eaten, so she tried to relax and let Ma fuss over her. It was a full hour later, and only after Bree had explained why she was sporting bruises, before she could broach the subject she really came to talk about.

The Andrews looked rather taken aback at Bree's first question. "How long have the two of you known Vic?"

Ma recovered first but stumbled over her words, "Why, Bree Darlin', whatever do ye mean? Vic's our son. We've known him all his life, o' course."

"Forgive me, Ma, but I know that isn't true. Vic confided in a friend of mine. She told me that you are like parents to him, but there is no blood relation; and yet you have the same last name. Please, this is not idle gossip or curiosity. I have very good reasons for wanting...needing to know. Won't you help me to understand?"

"Well, suppose ye tell us these good reasons," Pa said. "Then we'll decide what it is that ye might need to know."

Since she seemed to have no other choice, Bree spent the next few hours recounting for Ma and Pa her life with Grant, the years following his accident, and what had occurred in her life since she had met Vic. When she finished, the couple looked at each other, then back at Bree. Ma had tears in her eyes, and Pa seemed to have developed a nasty frog in his throat.

"Bree, Darlin', that's sure a sad story, especially the part about losing your faith in the Creator. We're real happy to hear you've found that again, though. So ye think you're in love with our Vic?"

"What?" The question startled Bree and quieted her for a moment. Love? Was that what this quest was about after all?

Was it possible that after all these years she had found someone she could love again? A man who could rival Grant for her heart?

When she looked back at Ma, Bree's eyes were not so dry either. "Yes, Ma, I believe that may be true. I hadn't really let myself be convinced of that until this moment. I've been too caught up in comparing him to Grant. I do know that when I'm with him and not wanting to strangle him, I feel secure and safe, feelings I only had when I was with Grant."

"But is that enough, and is that love?" Ma asked. "Is Vic man enough in yer eyes to replace Grant in yer heart? Still seems t' me ye might be interested in Vic 'cause he reminds ye of the first man ye ever loved. How can ye be certain what ye feel for Vic is love until ye can completely separate them? Vic's a wonderful man in his own right, and he deserves a woman who loves him for who he is now."

Bree didn't understand what Ma meant by "now," but she had to admit she was right about everything else she said.

"Oh, Ma, what am I going to do? You're right, I can't truly love Vic until I'm certain I've left Grant in the past. It's that at times...the way he looks at me...and some of the things he says....isn't there something you can tell me to help clear my mind of these misconceptions? I guess I haven't really given up hope that Grant is alive and Vic...is...Grant."

Bree was as shocked as Ma and Pa at the turn her thoughts had taken and the last came out in a whisper. But it was loud enough to cause Pa to jump up, put another log on the fire, and declare the conversation to be over.

"What's in Vic's past is fer him t' tell ye when the time is right. If he ain't told ye all ye want t' know yet, maybe ye ain't ready t' hear it. We've talked the whole day away now and not got a lick o' work done. You'll stay t' supper. Ma'll fix up yer bed and ye can start back in the mornin.' Be dark soon and cain't have ye wanderin' through these mountains alone when yer not used t' it. People git lost up here all the time."

Bree smiled, thinking she probably knew these mountains as well as Pa, but she didn't argue. Maybe they would think about what she'd asked and feel differently in the morning. Pa came to her and leaned down to give her a hug.

"We don't want t' seem mean, Bree. We love Vic, and we're startin' t' love you, too. Ever how this turns out, maybe you'd still come visit us some?"

Bree didn't think she could stand to see the Andrews if things didn't work out with Vic, but she couldn't hurt the old man.

"Sure, Pa. I'd love to see you both again." Bree suddenly remembered a comment Pa had made when she had first arrived. "Pa, what did you mean when I first got here today about having so much company?"

"Aw, some feller was lost up here a couple o' days ago. Don't know how tis people can always find us. We cain't even find our own way home sometimes." Bree knew that was an exaggeration. Both of the Andrews were still sharp as tacks.

"Anyways, Ma fed him then sent him on his way with good directions so's he wouldn't git turned around again. She'd asked if he wanted t' stay with us till Vic got here tomorrow so he could lead him back out, but he got all nervous-like and said he could find his way. He seemed awful curious about Vic, though. Started askin' lots of questions, kinda like ye done. That kinda got Ma riled, so she shooed him out the door as soon as she could, once he got so curious."

"Wait. Did you say Vic is coming tomorrow?" Bree asked in a panic.

"Sure, he always comes on Saturday. Tomorrow's Saturday ain't it?"

"Yes, it is." Bree had lost track of the days with all that had happened. "Pa, could you please make certain I'm up so I can leave before Vic gets here? I'm not ready to see him again just yet."

"Sure, sure, whatever you say, hon. Now let's get ye fed and t' bed or it'll be noon tomorrow afore ye even turn over."

# Chapter Seventeen

Something soft was caressing the side of Bree's face. In her dream she could see Grant lying beside her in their bed. His hand was brushing across her lips now. He was smiling just for her. She was smiling back as she struggled to wake up. Grant moved over her and began to kiss her awake. He kissed her forehead, her eyes, and slowly worked his way to her lips. He was holding her head between his hands as if he would never let her go, but it wasn't necessary. She had no intention of moving.

His thumbs were brushing the sides of her mouth and he was teasing her with feather light kisses. When she thought she would scream if he didn't increase the pressure, he did. It was at that moment that Bree realized she wasn't dreaming!

Her eyes flew open, and Grant's black eyes were staring lovingly into her hazel ones...no, not Grant's eyes...Vic's eyes. Vic was kissing her awake.

"Good morning, Little Lady."

Bree pushed Vic away, her feet hitting the floor so fast she sent him reeling off the bed.

"Why do you keep calling me that?" Bree demanded.

"As I've said before, if this is how you wake up I should have spared myself the discovery until I was in better shape." Vic was looking up at her from the floor, rubbing his elbow and looking for all the world like the cat that had found the canary. He was laughing as he asked, "Why do I call you what?"

"Little Lady. You called me Little Lady. And it isn't the first time, either. No one calls me that. No one except Grant."

Vic looked as disgusted as Bree was angry.

"Grant again. You know, most people only bury their dead once, but you keep digging yours up only to try and bury him again and again. I'm getting pretty tired of being the one who has to suffer to help you do it. Now, once and for all, enough."

Vic realized he was yelling at her and lowered his voice. "I'm sorry, Bree. Would you please get dressed and meet me outside? I have something very important to discuss with you. Something that in no way involves Grant."

With that said, Vic stormed out, leaving Bree with tears streaming down her face. How dare he be so cruel. Between Grant's memories and the reality that was Vic, she was coming apart. Ma was right. Something would have to give and soon.

She dressed quickly and went to find Vic. Ma was in the kitchen and couldn't quite meet Bree's eyes. She and Pa must have heard every word that had been said. Well, there was nothing she could do about that now. If they had made sure to wake her as she had asked, the whole scene could have been avoided anyway.

"Vic's on the back porch," Ma told her, without looking up.

She found Vic on the swing that overlooked the valley. He didn't hear her approach, so she leaned against the doorway and took a moment to study him while he was unaware of her. He wasn't scowling now as he admired the beauty around him, and she had to admit that although he wasn't Grant, he was equally handsome. If only she could wipe Grant from her mind, she could probably fall deeply in love with Vic. Vic's mood swings often seemed to be directly related to her talk of Grant. She would hope those would lessen if she could keep that subject in check. She still couldn't understand why the Lord didn't seem to be helping her with this. Maybe Vic wasn't the man for her and He was protecting her by keeping Grant in her mind.

As she walked over to sit on the swing with Vic, he looked at her and smiled. The morning sun was full in his face and the tiny scars that had baffled her from the start of this relationship were very evident. She began their conversation with an apology. She was probably going to have to do a lot of that until her relationship with the Lord was completely back on track.

"I'm sorry, Vic. I guess I don't wake up well with other people. I've slept alone for a long time now. In this day and age, I would probably be considered a virgin by most standards. There hasn't been a man in my life before or after Grant, so when you awakened me the way you did this morning, I couldn't seem to separate dream from reality. I honestly don't mean to hurt you but try as I might, I can't seem to get you and Grant to stay in different corners of my mind. Do you think you could forgive me yet again?"

"I can forgive you as often as I have to, Bree. I can do anything if it will keep you in my life. Leap tall buildings; hold back dams..."

Bree held up her hand to stop his declarations of heroics.

"Okay. I believe you." They both laughed, but Vic sobered quickly.

"I told you the other night that I love you and I don't turn my emotions on and off that easily, but this particular discussion can wait until another time."

Vic paused briefly, took a deep breath and began again. "Bree, I'm pretty sure I know who has been following you and assaulted you. He is probably also who has been causing all the problems I've been having at work."

"Vic, that's great! Who is it?"

"It may not be so great. Do you remember Brannon, the photographer I was using for the shoot we did together in Florida?"

"Of course. It isn't easy to forget someone who almost caused the death of a friend. Even if it wasn't intentional. Why do you ask about him?"

"I've been doing some checking and asking around the office, and I'm sorry, but I've also been asking around your office. He's been spotted both places on days when these things have occurred. You have a neighbor who gave the police a description of a man who had been hanging around your neighborhood lately. She recognized Brannon from a picture I showed her this morning before I headed up here. All roads seem to be leading to him. I notified the police and they are trying to locate him for questioning now."

"I don't understand, Vic. Why would Brannon want to hurt me, or you for that matter? People get fired all the time and they don't usually go around assaulting those responsible. And I didn't fire him. I had nothing to do with that decision. I'm afraid I don't understand why you think it would be him."

"Bree, there's more about Brannon that you don't know. I hired him as a favor for a trusted employee. He's her cousin. I was told that he was having difficulty finding work due to a medical disorder. I felt that he was being discriminated against, so I was happy to hire him. I was busy with a lot of projects at the time so I didn't ask for the usual references. When I found out Brannon's background was in photography, I gave him a couple of jobs and he did them very well. He showed no signs of disrespect or anything other than a great work ethic, until what happened with your girls.

"After I fired him and things started going wrong around the office, I started doing the checking I should have done before I hired him. I found out Brannon had served time in prison and also in a mental hospital. Bree, I can never apologize enough for the danger I have put you and others in by bringing Brannon into your life."

Bree couldn't believe Vic was taking responsibility for things Brannon had done.

"It isn't necessary to apologize, Vic. You had no way of knowing that helping out a person in need would turn out this way. I don't suppose it really matters, but do you know why Brannon was in jail?"

Vic turned away and was having difficulty formulating his response.

"He was originally jailed for assault, but...the woman he was accused of attacking...well...she died, but it couldn't be proven that it was from the injuries Brannon inflicted. He had a pretty good lawyer who was able to get him paroled early since it was a first offense. He had already been jailed for the assault charge before she died. I think the family of the victim is trying to appeal, but in the meantime Brannon is free to go wherever he pleases. But Bree, it gets worse. No one can locate Brannon now, and other than your neighbor who thinks they've seen him around your house, no one has seen him for days. He hasn't been to his usual hangouts and his cousin says he's disappeared."

"Do you trust the cousin to be honest with you about that?"

"I do. She has been with me a long time and appreciated that I tried to help Brannon. She didn't know about his past either. Apparently lying was part of who he was. I'm so happy we got you and the girls out of Florida when we did. There is no telling what might have happened if they had stayed there for another night. It was bad enough as it was."

He took Bree's hands in his. "I'm responsible for all of this, Bree. I don't want you alone until Brannon is caught. If he is the man who attacked you, you could be in real danger. I think he's probably a killer whether he's been convicted of it or not. For some reason known only to him, he seems to blame the two of us for his problems, mostly you. I have hired a detective to watch over you if you'll allow it. I'd stay with you myself, but I think I know how well you'd accept that."

He looked so hopeful, but Bree knew her renewed convictions wouldn't allow that.

"You're right about that. We can't live together. I suppose having a detective around might be okay, for a short while. But what about you, Vic? Don't you think you're in danger too?"

"So far Brannon hasn't attacked me physically. I don't understand it, but I think you're the one he most wants to harm. Maybe it's because he's found out how much you mean to me. Or maybe he thinks you convinced me to fire him. Could be because he's actually a coward and you make an easier target. Or maybe he's crazy. Whatever the reason, I believe you are still in harm's way."

Vic paused to take in the beauty surrounding the cabin. "You know, sometimes I wish I had never left this cabin. Life was so simple here. But then I would have never met you. Come on, let's get some tea and biscuits."

He started to rise, but Bree restrained him with a hand on his arm. She could feel the vibrancy of the man and saw his reaction to her touch. Maybe she could try once more to probe him for the answers she wanted. Maybe in his concern for her he would be open with her now.

"Why did you, Vic? Leave, I mean. Why leave such beauty and simplicity to move to the city and get involved in business and finance if you didn't have to?" Inside she was pleading, *"Please, please, Vic. Tell me now. Tell me the truth."*

He must have sensed somehow that this would be her final plea, that if he didn't tell her now what she thought she wanted to hear, he might lose her for good. Bree saw in his eyes the moment he made his choice.

Vic began slowly, but the longer he talked the faster the words came, until when he finished Bree could tell he was exhausted as well as relieved to have finally shared this with her. And she was thrilled with what he had revealed.

"It all started about four years ago." Bree realized Vic's story began about the time she had lost Grant. She sat quietly as Vic continued.

"Pa had been out on his monthly tour checking for anything out of the ordinary when he came across a young man lying in a field not too far from the cabin. The man's clothes were nearly shredded to bits, he was suffering from shock and had lacerations and burns over most of his body, especially his face. He was dehydrated and disoriented. He couldn't tell Pa who he was or how he'd come to be there.

"Pa thought he was a hiker who had been attacked by a bear, but when he examined the cuts more closely he knew they hadn't been made by an animal. He managed to load the man up on his wagon, I'm still not sure how he did that, and got him back to the cabin where Ma tended him until they could get help.

"Pa radioed the closest Cades Cove park ranger who got a medical chopper to them in record time. The young man was almost completely unresponsive by then.

"Ma and Pa had lost a son many years before who would have been about the same age this man looked, so they sought to protect their new charge. They pulled out their son's birth certificate and claimed the man was their son. The young man was so badly injured no one could tell it wasn't the same man in the latest photo the couple had. Ma and Pa felt that the Lord had sent them a son to replace the one they had lost years before, so they lied for the first time in their lives.

"They told the paramedics that the young man was their son who had been born with special needs. He had stumbled back to the cabin a short time after leaving for a hike. They had no idea what had happened to him. The paramedics were more interested in saving his life than questioning the elderly couple.

"The man had quite a few broken bones and such extensive injuries that it took multiple major surgeries, plastic and otherwise, and months of recovery before he could be released from the hospital. The surgeon had no recent pictures of Ma and Pa's son to go by so he did reconstruction as best he could. It never occurred to anyone to question if the Andrews were telling the truth. Why would it?

"Ma and Pa brought the young man back here when he was discharged from the hospital and cared for him until he fully recovered, almost an entire year. The Andrews were always up front with him about how he came to be here. They thought that might help him remember who he was. But to this day he has never recovered his memories.

"What happened to that man in the woods is as much a mystery to me as to everyone else. You see, Bree, I was and am that man. And the worst of it is that I have no memory of anything before I woke up in the hospital after the surgery, not my early life or the recent life right before the Andrews found me. I don't know how I was injured, how long I had been in these mountains or why, before Pa came along. Everything about my past life is gone...so...I am the man you see before you, no more, no less.

"Bree, I know something about me reminds you of your late husband but surely you understand now that it would be impossible for me to be him." Vic looked at her expectantly, thinking she had to admit now that he was right. As usual, Bree surprised him.

She had been listening so intently that she had pressed her nails into her palms and drawn blood. She reached out to Vic with tears in her eyes, knowing without a doubt now that the man before her was Grant. But how was she going to convince him?

"Vic, all you have said has convinced me even more that you have to be Grant. He disappeared exactly when you appeared. He was lost here in the Smokies. You appeared, out of nowhere, here in the Smokies. You seem to be close to the same age. Some of the passengers survived the plane crash. Your injuries could have easily been caused by a plane crash. Though I never saw Grant without his beard, you are very similar in all of your features, even after the extensive surgery. Your size is the same and when we're together, the way I feel is the same if I would admit to it. Don't you see? You have to be Grant! Won't you at least consider the possibility?"

"Bree, I love you and want you to love me for who I am, not who you want me to be. I consider the Andrews my parents since I can recall no others, and they love me like their own son. It took me nearly a year to fully recover. I knew I couldn't hide here forever. Something drove me to leave and get back out into the real world. Ma and Pa had a small fortune stashed away. They convinced me to take what I needed to start my own business. I found I had a good head for finance and it didn't take long for me to pay Ma and Pa back. I acquired some small companies as they became available and have amassed a considerable amount of capital in the last three years. I invested in stocks for the Andrews so they can live comfortably now wherever they are.

"I haven't recovered any portion of my memory since the accident, and the doctors tell me the longer I go, the less likely it is that I will. Even if what you believe is true, I have no memory of you and your years with Grant. Can't you forget him and love me for me...just me? Not some memory you've held onto for years?"

Bree shook her head and replied sadly, "Vic, I'm so sorry but I don't think we have anything else to discuss. It's very clear to me that you could be Grant and very obvious that you disagree. I can't look at you and not see him. You can't spend time with me without expecting me to forget about him. It breaks my heart to say this, but I think we should stop seeing each other, at least for a while."

"I don't agree that we should stop seeing each other, Bree. I love you so much my heart hurts when we're apart. I'm not sure how to live without you now that we've found each other. But if I can't change your mind, I will try my best to abide by your decision.

"I am Vic Andrews. Until you can separate me from Grant, I suppose I will have to agree that we should each go our own way and try to work this out for ourselves. But please, Bree, if you ever manage to get Grant out of your heart, please come find me. I'll make sure you always know how to reach me."

Broken-hearted, Bree went back into the house. Ma and Pa were sitting quietly next to the fireplace. Both had tears streaming down their face and Bree supposed they had heard at least part of what she and Vic had talked about. They looked as sad as she felt. In spite of how it might add to their misery, Bree still had to ask one last question before she left.

"Why did you do it?" Bree asked them.

They looked confused by her question.

"Did it never occur to you that the man you rescued might have a family? That there might be someone whose heart you would break by not admitting how you found him? How could you be so selfish? What you did was practically kidnapping. I lost Grant because of the two of you years ago, and now I'm losing Vic because I can't get him to agree to the possibility that he might be Grant. Please, help me to understand why you did what you did when you found him. Please explain why you lied."

Bree was in tears, and Ma and Pa were crying right along with her.

"We didn't mean no harm," Ma said, barely able to get the words out. "Pa and I never gave it no thought. There was no weddin' band, no wallet, and the young man had no idea who he was. We thought we could give him a good life. The life our son would have had if he had lived."

"We're sorry, Bree, for the heartache we've put you through if Vic is really who you think he is," Pa said. "But t' be honest, you don't really know that."

"It doesn't matter who Vic really is," Bree said. "What you did was wrong on all levels. I don't know if I can ever forgive you."

Vic walked in on the last part of their conversation. His dejected look said it all.

"I don't know who to feel the most sorry for," he told them. "The woman who is walking out of my life due to her own stubbornness, or the couple who are coming to view her as a future daughter-in-law and are seeing their dreams dashed; or myself." Vic turned to Bree as he continued. "I have never felt any ill will toward the Andrews for what they did on my behalf, and I'm not going to start now. Instead, I've always been grateful. I would have died if not for them."

Vic made one last attempt to draw Bree into his arms. "I have to believe that you will realize your mistake and come around to my point of view soon. You have to. As I said before, I don't know if I can live without you, now that I've had you in my life."

Bree struggled away, her eyes so full of tears she could barely see, but refusing to be swayed. Her mind was made up.

Bree also refused Vic's offer to walk her to her car. She had been so sure Vic was Grant and that she could convince him of that. But it hadn't worked.

If she had to get over Grant, again, she may as well start immediately and do it alone, as she had done before. This time she would have God's help because she wasn't going to close Him out again. She didn't understand why Vic was being so stubborn about this. Maybe he was right and she was the stubborn one. Maybe God wanted her in Vic's life right now. She needed to step back and spend some time in prayer to figure out which way to proceed.

The first time Grant had disappeared from her life, it had been almost impossible to deal with. Getting over Grant the second time around was going to be even more difficult.

# Chapter Eighteen

A couple of weeks later Bree realized it was Vic she was struggling to get over. Crazy as it was, without Vic around she thought less and less about Grant and more about Vic. She wasn't sure if she had reached the point where she could love him for who he was and leave Grant completely in the past, but she knew she was going to have to try because life like this was miserable.

She felt the Lord was leading her toward Vic, but she didn't want to be the one to make the first call. She knew she was being stubborn, but what if he had forgotten about her altogether? True to his word, he had not pressed her, or attempted to see her since their tearful goodbye at the cabin. How much in love could he possibly be if he could go this long and not even try to get in touch with her? But hadn't she done the same thing?

She might be in love with Vic, but how would she feel if she was actually with him again? What if she made the call and they started seeing each other again only to have her memories come between them like before? A person could go crazy trying to figure this out!

Bree wondered if Glory was still spending time with Vic, but she was too proud to ask her. After everything that had transpired between them, Vic may have put Bree out of his mind and taken Glory up on her offer to be more than a friend. That thought always made her cringe. Even though it might seem impossible for her and Vic to work things out, she wasn't sure she could handle knowing he was with someone else.

Bree had been so miserable for so long it was beginning to show, both in her face and in her concentration. Her business had suddenly become much less important to her and her faith and personal life had taken on new meaning. Why couldn't she accept that the Lord was working in her life and call Vic as she felt led to do? Maybe he was as miserable as she was, but that was a terrible thing to wish on someone.

Surprisingly she no longer felt like she was being watched, and the man who had attacked her, whether it was Brannon or not, seemed to have disappeared. Bree knew in her heart that the Lord had taken care of it and she refused to worry about it. She had also decided that neither Vic nor Chris could have been involved as she had first suspected.

She had run into Chris at a local coffee shop. He had introduced the woman with him as his fiancé. He seemed happy and even apologized to Bree for his past behavior before they parted.

Once again all Bree had left was her work. Attempting to focus on that was a losing battle. Bree was making mistakes at every turn and, even worse, had begun snapping at her employees, something she had never done. Bree was certain that if she didn't change her frame of mind, and quickly, Kathy would soon look for work elsewhere.

More than ever she was thinking of taking Cal's advice and merging her company with Vic's. Cal had told her that he had had no contact with Vic, but the offer had not been withdrawn either. The merger could possibly solve some issues but would probably create a whole lot more. It would definitely require that she and Vic talk, but Bree didn't want his attention in that way.

Disgusted with her indecision, Bree threw down her pen and walked to the window. It was an evening much like the one when Vic made his first appearance in her office.

As Bree stretched, she heard her door open and had such a feeling of déjà vu that she turned expectantly, certain that it would be Vic entering her office once again.

She was disappointed and surprised when she saw Glory hesitating nervously in her doorway. Things had been awkward between them lately, and Bree had been careful to avoid extensive contact with the model. She knew it wasn't very Christian of her. She missed her friend. But seeing Glory brought back memories of Vic, so Bree had chosen the easy path by staying away from Glory's shoots.

Glory appeared as uncomfortable as Bree felt. "Bree, I'm sorry to disturb you...Kathy wasn't at her desk and I need to talk to you...I've been wanting to see you. Not just because I've missed you as a friend, but...I really need to tell you something. It's about Vic."

Bree was pretty sure she knew what Glory was about to tell her. She didn't want to hear that Vic was pursuing Glory, or that they were seeing each other. She knew it was most likely true, but her heart couldn't stand to hear it put into words, not yet. Bree started shaking her head as she reached for her coat.

"Glory, I'm sure you know that Vic and I are no longer seeing each other, in a business, or personal way, so I can't imagine why we would need to talk about him."

"I know that, Bree, that's why it's taken me this long to come to you...to tell you...I think Vic would want you to know...just in case. I mean, I'm sure he wouldn't want you to feel badly if something should happen and you never got to see him again."

Bree stopped with one arm in her coat as she turned back to the distraught model.

"What are you trying to say, Glory? Is there something wrong with Vic?"

Tears were rolling down Glory's face as she tried to explain.

"Bree, the Andrews called Kathy last week and she called me. She didn't think she should bother you with this. You had told her you and Vic broke up, and that you weren't taking any calls from him, or about him. Bree, Vic's been hurt. I didn't tell you sooner because I thought he was strong and would be okay, but the doctors say that the longer he lingers in this condition, well...it's been two weeks, and the doctors aren't sure how he'd be now, even if he did come out of the coma."

"Coma! Glory, you're telling me Vic has been in a coma for two weeks and no one has said a word to me. Where is he? Never mind. You can tell me the rest in the car. Come on. You're taking me to him."

As they drove to the hospital Glory relayed all the details to Bree. "A couple of weeks ago, Vic was returning from the mountains and was intentionally run off the road by a man driving a large truck. There were witnesses. One of them said the accident had to have been deliberate. He saw the man driving the truck jerk his wheel in Vic's direction and hit him in the side. Vic's car had hit a tree with such force that Vic's seat belt broke and he was thrown into the windshield. Among other injuries he suffered a concussion. The doctors didn't think it was too serious at first, but as days went by and Vic didn't wake up, they began to look for another cause for the coma. So far, the doctors have found no medical reason for Vic's condition, and as time passes, they become more and more concerned.

"The doctors told me earlier today that the longer Vic stays in the coma, the less the chance for a full recovery, especially a recovery without serious impairment. His heart actually stopped a few days ago. He was revived and they have him on life support now. That's why I decided I had to come and tell you. Vic loves you so much. I don't understand why you chose to break his heart. I know you're a good person. I guess you had your reasons. But if I had a man like Vic who loved me the way he loves you, well..." Glory was so tearful she couldn't finish.

Bree was sure she had never felt worse in her life. Glory was right. Vic had done nothing to her but declare his love her and Bree had practically thrown that love back in his face.

"I know that something went wrong in our friendship and I'm not sure what that was. I hope you can put that aside and we can be friends again. But mostly because I think Vic needs all his friends and family around right now."

This brought tears to Bree's eyes as well. She reached over and took Glory's right hand in hers, wondering how someone so young could have so much wisdom.

"I'm sorry, Glory. I should never have let anything come between our friendship no matter what was going on in my life. Can you forgive me?"

Glory squeezed her hand. "Of course, Bree. We'll talk soon. But first you need to see the man who loves you and who, if I'm not mistaken, you love right back."

When Glory pulled up to the hospital, Bree was out of the car almost before it stopped, reaching Vic's room in record time and telling her heart to calm down before she entered.

The thought of seeing Vic again eliminated any possibility of that, no matter his present condition.

The first person Bree saw when she entered Vic's room was Ma. She was sitting in a corner chair and looked years older than when Bree had last seen her. She rose, coming to Bree and embracing her as though no time had passed since their last meeting. Her tear-streaked cheeks made Bree wonder if she was too late and there had been more bad news.

"I'm so glad ye finally came, Bree honey. When ye didn't come right away, we realized ye must have gotten over Vic better than he was gonna git over you. He didn't stop talking about ye right up till he left the day of the accident. He kept on thinkin' you'd be back. Even talked t' God about it. He knew ye had a special relationship with the Lord, and he wanted that for hisself. At first, because he thought it would get him closer t' ye, but durin' his prayer askin' God t' bring ye back t' him, the Lord touched Vic's heart and changed him. Vic believes in Jesus now as his Savior. No matter what happens now we know Vic will be okay. But I don't understand, Bree, why ain't ye come before now? Don't ye love our Vic no more?"

Bree was excited to hear about Vic's conversion, but she was also concerned that Ma and Pa thought she really didn't have feelings for Vic.

"Ma, I didn't know about Vic's accident until today. I don't blame her, but Kathy never told me you called. Glory just told me today and I came immediately! You must believe I would have been here if I had known."

"How could ye not know? Vic's well known in this town, and the reporters ain't stopped comin' around ever day. The way the two o' ye parted...well...we weren't sure...especially about yer feelins' fer us."

"Ma, please believe me. I haven't watched the news or picked up a paper since I left your cabin. I've tried to keep busy so I wouldn't have time to think about Vic. I understand if you harbor ill feelings for me after the way we parted, but please, please, forgive me. I wasn't thinking clearly the last time I saw you and I hope to make things right with you and Pa."

Ma couldn't speak through her tears and gave Bree a strong hug instead.

"Please, Ma. May I see Vic now? Will you and Pa be okay with that?"

Bree was worried that Ma would be angry at her still, and even though it would break her heart, she wouldn't insist on seeing Vic if Ma didn't want her to.

"Of course, darlin'. Pa and me, we've been prayin' ye'd have a change of heart and come. We've asked the Lord t' forgive us fer what we did t' you, and Vic. We didn't mean no harm. You were right. It were selfish of us and we cain't even begin t' repay either of ye for the heartache we've caused.

"We think Vic don't care if he lives if it has t' be without ye. That's why he don't wake up. Maybe with ye here now, he'll hear ye and want t' come back t' us, I mean, t' ye. Please try t' bring him back. Even if the two of ye decide never t' see us again, just knowin' yer t'gether would make us happy. His bed is on t' other side of the curtain."

Bree had doubts that her presence would be the one to reach Vic after the way they had parted, but she would certainly try. She pulled back the curtain and gasped aloud when she got her first view of him. It wasn't the tubes and machines that sent her into a state of shock. It was his face, or what she could see of it.

Vic had apparently not been shaved since the accident and now, sporting a full beard and mustache, he was the spitting image of Grant. Her heart turned over in her chest and she was suddenly no longer sure which man to pray for in this new circumstance. Bree's knees began to weaken and she would surely have collapsed had Ma not slid a chair under her as she went down. Bree didn't reveal to the older woman that thoughts of Grant were the true reason for her weakness.

"Ma...he looks terrible. He's...really bad, isn't he?"

"It surely does look that way, but we ain't give up hope, and don't ye dare neither."

Bree looked again at Vic and decided right then that with the Lord's help, she would pull him through this. She had lost one man she loved. Regardless of who this man was, she loved him and refused to lose him, too. Yes. She finally admitted to herself. She loved Vic, and when he awakened she would tell him so.

# Chapter Nineteen

The initial shock of seeing Vic eventually passed, and Bree set up a constant vigil at his bedside, refusing to leave except for absolute necessities. His doctors and nurses soon realized they were stuck with her and allowed her to come or go as she pleased. The medical personnel didn't seem to share her faith that Vic would pull through. That may have been part of the reason they saw no problem in letting her stay.

Once they learned that she was a permanent fixture at Vic's bedside, someone started having a tray brought to her at mealtimes. Otherwise Bree would never have eaten anything. It became obvious to Bree in just a few days that the doctors were allowing her time with Vic because they didn't really believe he would ever leave the hospital. In her heart, Bree had to believe differently.

She had bathed the situation in prayer and believed beyond any doubt that the Lord was going to let Vic live. She had to convince Vic of that, so she began having one-sided conversations with him as if he could hear her, not caring who might be in the room.

She would speak to him as though they were having a normal chat, telling him about everyone who came and went throughout the day and why. It never occurred to her that for once she had total control of the conversation. That would have struck her as funny had her heart not been breaking.

"You know, Vic, we never got to take our hike. I know you're sure that I could out-climb you. But don't you think pretending to be asleep is taking the competition a bit far?"

Bree would squeeze his hand as she spoke to him but so far had not received a response.

"I've been thinking a lot about our merger. I've decided it might work. We do need to decide on a name for our new company. I'm happy to come up with that on my own, but I'd be happy to give you a say in that."

Still no response.

Bree couldn't stop thinking about the way she and Vic had parted. If she hadn't been so stubborn, they might have been able to work out their differences and Vic might not be in this condition today. But she knew the Lord had a plan, and Bree was staying right by Vic's side until that plan was revealed to her. She now completely believed that she and Vic were meant to be together, and nothing or no one, was going to sway her from that belief.

Bree heard footsteps behind her and turned to see Ma and Pa enter the room. Another month had passed since Bree had found out about Vic. Every day that went by with no sign of improvement from Vic seemed to age the Andrews incredibly. Bree knew their faith was every bit as strong as hers, probably stronger, but this constant vigil was taking a toll on them all.

Bree had set up an office of sorts next to Vic's bed and had been keeping up with her work from the room as well as helping out with Vic's company. For the most part though, she had left her company, and Smoky, in the capable hands of Cal and Kathy, communicating with them by phone and email. But she knew Cal couldn't continue his law practice and keep her afloat for much longer, even with all of Kathy's help. It was too much to ask from a man who had already been such a great friend.

Bree hugged the Andrews. "There hasn't been any change," she told them. "As you probably know, Vic had a living will, so the doctors removed all life support earlier this morning. Surprisingly, Vic is breathing fine on his own. His bodily functions seem to be fine, but he still isn't waking up."

Ma looked more concerned for Bree than Vic at the moment. "Bree, darlin' ye don't look well at all. The nurses told us ye ain't set a foot outside this room since we was here last week. Why don't ye take a short walk? Even just down the hall? Pa and I will stay right here and one of us will come git ye if there's any change. We promise."

Bree was touched by their concern, but she knew her place was with Vic. She had been telling him that for weeks, and she wasn't going to leave now and risk him waking up while she was gone. And she had to believe with all her heart that he was going to wake up.

"Thank you both for caring so much about me, but I hope you understand that I can't leave. I want to be the first person Vic sees when he wakes up, even if I'm not the person he wants to see. I want to tell him how much I love him and how sorry I am for trying to force him to be someone else. I have so much I want to say to him. I've been saying it all month, but I don't know if he hears me. I keep thinking maybe he can, so I keep telling him we're all here waiting for him, and we'll continue to be here until he's ready to come back. Sometimes I want to scream at him to wake up, but I realize that wouldn't help."

Bree looked back at Vic and touched his cheek as she leaned over to give him a gentle kiss on the lips. A single tear rolled down her face and fell on his cheek. If he had been able to see her at that moment, he could have never doubted the love shining in her eyes.

Ma sniffled behind her as Bree wiped the tear from Vic's cheek and rose up. She determined that she had to pull herself together for the sake of these two precious people who were beginning to mean almost as much to her as her own parents had.

"So, tell me how the two of you have been. Tell me about our mountains. It feels like years since I've seen them. Have you had any more strangers show up at your doorstep?"

Bree tried to take a shot at normal conversation and Ma and Pa looked grateful. But they had something else they wanted to talk about.

"Ye know, Bree, there's the strangest thing. Remember the young man we told ye about that got lost right before yer last visit?" At Bree's nod, Pa continued. "Well the police asked Ma and me t' go look at the feller that ran Vic off the road. They thought maybe we could tell 'em who he was and why he done what he done. Seems he weren't wearin' no seatbelt and was thrown outa his truck. They couldn't find nothin' with his name or any I.D. He was in a room down the hall. He was in awful shape, worse than Vic. He never came to while we was in his room. We kinda think he was the young man who was at the cabin the same weekend ye came. It was hard t' tell on account he was so beat up from the wreck.

"One of the nurses thought she recognized him from bein' here before. She ust' t' work in the ward where they treat the people what have mental problems. She told 'em a name. Once they got t' checkin' the hospital records and ran some tests they found out it was the same man."

Bree had never heard Pa talk for so long, and was shocked by this new information.

"You mean the man that ran Vic off the road…he was here?"

"Yep. Witnesses at the accident said it looked like he hit Vic on purpose but then lost control of his own vehicle. Ma and me, we felt real sorry for him, even after what he did. He only had this one gal who come t' see him. We started goin' t' visit him whenever we come here. Turned out his name was Brannon. Don't recollect his first name though."

"Brannon! Are you sure, Pa?" Bree asked.

"Well o' course I'm sure. I may be old but I ain't senile!"

Ma interrupted. "Why, Bree? Is it important t' know his name?"

"Brannon is the one who caused Vic so many problems, and managed to sabotage some of Vic's business deals. Vic believed that he was the man who had been following me, and who assaulted me, twice. This would explain why no one has seen or heard from him in so long. Apparently, his hatred for Vic and me was deeper than anyone realized, but to actually try and kill Vic, he must have been more unstable than anyone knew."

"Yeah, that's what everone around here was sayin' once they decided who he was. We've been wonderin' if things would have been different if we'd told Vic about him comin' t' the cabin. His visit seemed innocent enough, but if we had told Vic before he left that day maybe he would have been payin' more attention and woulda been more careful goin' home."

"Are you telling me that the last day Vic and I were at the cabin together is the day this happened?"

At the Andrews' nods, Bree laid her head down on Vic's bed and began crying in earnest. All the tears she had refused to shed over the last few weeks finally came to the surface. It was clear to her now that she had been the true cause of Vic's accident. If his mind had been on driving, instead of preoccupied with their discussion, the accident would probably not have happened. Vic was too sharp and alert when he was driving for Brannon to have caused him to wreck, unless his thoughts were on some spoiled girl who insisted on having everything her own way!

"Would you like t' come see him with us now?" This from Ma.

"Wait. You mean he's still here? He didn't die?"

"Die? No. He was on the mend when we saw him last week."

"It sounded like you were talking about him in the past tense. Yes. I believe I would like to see him."

Bree could feel her anger rising with thoughts of seeing Brannon again. Her worldly self wanted nothing more than to be mad at him for what he had done to Glory, to her, and now to Vic. But she knew she had to control that.

Ma and Pa led her down the hall before stopping to knock on a door only three over from Vic. A feminine voice quietly invited them in.

Bree stepped through first and recognized Brannon instantly. He looked a lot less intimidating in his present condition than she remembered him from the beach and appeared to be sleeping. The woman at his bedside stood to greet them.

"Hello Mr. and Mrs. Andrews." The young woman greeted them warmly and looked at Bree.

"This is Vic's …well she's our…." Bree saw that Ma was struggling to introduce her so she reached for the woman's hand.

"I'm Brianna Walters. Vic and I are business acquaintances."

The woman shook her hand in greeting as the group stepped into the hall.

"I know who you are Ms. Walters. Dave Brannon is my cousin. I'm Vic's assistant, Nancy Felling. You and I have spoken by phone. I owe you an apology, along with so many other people. When I begged Mr. Andrews to hire him I had no idea what my cousin was capable of. It's terrible what he has done to so many good people. I hope you can forgive me for the role I played in all of this."

Nancy was in tears and Bree felt all of her anger melt away as she reached to hug her. Yes, Brannon had caused some terrible things to happen, but it looked like he was paying a price as well. And it was not Bree's place to judge. If Ma and Pa could forgive Brannon, she certainly could do the same.

"How is your cousin doing?" Bree was surprised to find that she really did care.

"Oh, he is doing so much better. He will probably be released into police custody soon. I am so happy he didn't die. I hope the Lord will give him an opportunity to redeem himself for the bad things he's done. I know he has done real harm but he is the only family I have left. I do care for him in spite of his temperament."

"Of course you love him, Nancy. I wouldn't expect otherwise. He's lucky to have you. It's been wonderful to meet you, but we need to get back to Vic now. I would hate for him to wake up and none of us is there."

"Of course, Ms. Walters. Thank you for coming to see us and for your kindness and forgiveness. Is it okay if I ask that you pray for my cousin? As you know, he really needs it."

"It would be my pleasure, Nancy. Please stay in touch. You know how to reach me."

The three moved back to Vic's room. Bree was torn between her feelings that it wasn't fair that Brannon should be healed and getting out of the hospital when there was still no assurance that Vic would even live. She tried her best to quiet those thoughts. But once back in Vic's room, the dam that had been holding back Bree's tears broke once again.

She laid her head on Vic's chest, wanting to pound on it instead while demanding that he open his eyes and talk to her. Her eyes filled and her heart broke all over again. She was going to have to come to terms with the fact that Vic might never go home. She knew that now. She only hoped that she could forgive Brannon if Vic didn't survive.

Bree's sobs were getting totally out of control, but she couldn't seem to stop herself from pouring out her grief. Feeling a shaking hand begin to stroke her hair, she looked up, expecting to see Ma beside her. Ma and Pa had moved to the other side of the bed and tears were streaming down their faces as well, and they were looking at Vic. Bree looked too, and beautiful black eyes were looking right back at her.

"Hello, Little Lady," was all Vic could say in a hoarse voice before it broke completely, and he was crying right along with them. He pulled her closer and pressed his face into the side of her neck as he took a deep breath. "Ah. There's the scent I love."

Bree reached for the nurses' button, jabbing it repeatedly while clinging to Vic. She, Ma and Pa were all nearly in his bed when the nurse arrived a few seconds later.

When she saw that her patient was conscious, the nurse tried to shoo them all out of the room as she paged the doctor.

Vic, however, refused to let go of Bree's hand until both she and the Andrews promised to wait right outside the door. Reluctantly they agreed to leave the room as first one, then a slew of doctors rushed through the door.

Bree, Ma, and Pa waited teary-eyed for the next hour while watching doctor after doctor enter Vic's room, only now their tears were tears of joy. They were crying and praying and thanking God.

When another hour had passed and not a single physician had come back out of Vic's room, their joy changed to concern. Bree decided to find out for herself what was going on.

She pushed on Vic's door just as it opened from inside and Dr. Massey, the same doctor who had treated her, came out looking baffled. Bree couldn't quite form the words to ask the question and she wasn't sure she wanted to hear the answer.

Pa, however, had no such qualms. "Now looky here young man, what have you people been doin' in there for the last couple o' hours? If there's some problem with Vic you should have been out here tellin' us afore now! So spit it out!"

Dr. Massey was not taken aback one bit by the outburst and looked instead at Bree, "He's asking for you."

Bree was halfway through the door, but the doctor held her back.

"Ms. Walters, there's something you should know first."

At the troubled look in Bree's eyes, the doctor tried to reassure her, as he pulled the door closed once again.

"It's nothing physical. Vic seems fully functional. He's weak of course, but for what he's been through, he's in marvelous condition physically."

"So what's the problem, Doc?" Pa interrupted.

"Well," the doctor was still hesitating, "He can answer most of my questions correctly. All of his reflexes test out, his memory seems intact, there is this one thing."

"Oh, for Pete's sake, doc, what are ye tryin' t' say?" Pa insisted.

"Well, we keep calling him Vic, or Mr. Andrews, and he keeps insisting he is someone named Grant Walters. Is that a relative of yours, Ms. Walters?"

Bree was no longer listening. She had headed back into the room, Ma and Pa close on her heels, but she couldn't see Vic for all the people surrounding his bed. She could, however, hear his voice, and though he was hoarse, he was already taking charge.

"Would someone please get my wife in here? She was here just a while ago and I'm sure she wouldn't leave. And there's Ma and Pa…"

He stopped when he saw Bree hovering at the foot of his bed and opened his arms to her. She needed no further encouragement. The entourage of medical professionals parted to let her through and she was in his embrace in a second. Looking into his eyes, Bree saw that they were clear and he did not appear at all confused about who she was, or who he was.

He pulled her head down for a kiss that shook her to her toes. She kissed him right back, not caring that the room was full of people who were watching them intently. This time Bree was the first to break the contact.

"I'm mighty glad to have you back," she told him and continued before he could respond, "I have one question. Who are you?"

She heard the gasps of those in the room with them but didn't care, this was too important. The answer she was about to receive would set the course for the rest of her life.

"You can ask that question of the man you promised to love and honor above all others until death?" He glanced over at the closest nurse who giggled in response to his next query. "How quickly they forget, huh?"

"Grant?" Bree breathed out his name barely above a whisper. She had made up her mind to love Vic and she certainly didn't want to make another mistake at this point. "Grant, is it really you?"

"It's really me, Little Lady, and I remember everything. I even remember the time I spent as Vic Andrews. I sure am glad I got my memory back before I convinced you to marry that cad!"

Bree felt her eyes filling with tears once again, but Grant was having none of that. He reached for her hand to remove his wedding band from her thumb. Bree watched through her tears as he tried to place it back on his ring finger. With the tape still wrapped around the band, he couldn't get it past the first knuckle.

"Thanks for holding on to this for me, but I seem to remember it fitting a bit better."

Grant was quick to try and stop Bree's tears. "Now you listen here, I've been without you for four years, and I refuse to waste another second of either of our lives making you unhappy. I think I did enough of that as Vic Andrews. Good grief, Bree, it's a wonder I didn't drive you crazy, insisting I was Vic when you were so convinced I was Grant. But you, you never gave up on me, did you?"

Bree shook her head, unable to speak as he continued.

"I'm so glad you didn't. It made me furious when I was Vic, but now that I'm myself again I realize how much you must have loved me to have held on for so long…and how much you still do. I know that God has brought us back together, and your faith in Him helped make that possible. I know you struggled for a while, and so did I, but we can regain what we had before with His help. Are you with me?"

Bree still couldn't find her voice, so she was showing Grant how much she still loved him with her actions when a gentle hand nudged her shoulder. Ma and Pa were beside her looking very unsure of themselves. She had regained her husband, but they must feel as though they had lost another son. She could tell by their worried frowns that they were afraid there would be no place for them in the life of this man. Grant could read their uncertainty and pulled Ma toward him for a big hug as he grabbed Pa's hand.

"I owe a great deal to both of you, and also an apology for all I've put you through as well. I know that I wouldn't be here today were it not for the two of you so please, if you're willing, I would very much like to remain a part of your lives. I love you both like my own parents, and you will probably be seeing a lot more of me and my wife than before if you're okay with that."

Ma and Pa were so emotional nodding was all they could do.

"As a matter of fact, if I could get all these people to clear out, Bree and I could get to work on a godchild for you. What do you say, Little Lady?"

And there it was, that lopsided grin that she had come to love with Vic and now could keep with Grant.

Bree blushed to her roots, but Pa chimed in before she could answer.

"Oh no ye don't! None o' that hanky panky till ye make an honest woman out o' Bree. Ma and me'll git the church booked as soon as yer able t' git outta that bed, and you won't be layin' a hand on the gal till then."

Grant held up both hands in surrender. "Okay, okay! You do realize that legally we're still married, right?" And there was that bear of a laugh Bree had missed so much.

Grant was asking the question of the Andrews, but he was looking at Bree. Only after she nodded did Grant agree with Pa's demand. But he had a question for her as well.

"Bree, I can't get down on my knees yet but what do you say, Little Lady? Would you do me the honor of renewing our vows to make this old goat happy?" He was referring to Pa, but the old man took no offense.

"Maybe then you could see your way clear to start a family with an old mountain man who's come back from the grave." Grant's eyes twinkled. Bree knew he was confident there was no way she would refuse.

"Oh, I think there's a 'ghost' of a chance this could work out. After all, you've never broken a promise to me yet," Bree agreed.

She moved back into Grant's arms where she belonged. She never heard Pa as he started telling all the medical personnel still in the room how he never doubted for a minute these two would work things out.

Ma smiled and said a prayer of thanks to her Maker.

*Epilogue*

Bree and Grant were on the west porch of their now completed dream home, watching as the sun made a final effort before fading behind the ridge. As Grant had promised, they had renewed their vows in the Primitive Baptist Church in Cades Cove the day after he was released from the hospital. The Andrews had insisted on hosting a reception at their cabin.

Family, friends and business associates had maxed out the few seats in the hundred plus year old building. It was the third week of October and there was no better time to be in the Great Smoky Mountains. Colors on the trees were so vivid it was blinding. The blue sky above her beloved mountains was right out of a painting, only better because it was real. Bree knew only God could create a blue so ethereal.

She and Grant had snuck away from the crowd to pray before the ceremony. Bree had never heard a sweeter prayer.

Grant's voice broke as he spoke to his Maker. "Father God, I can barely form the words to tell You how grateful I am that You brought Bree back into my life. Thank You for watching over her while I was unable to do that. I pray that Your love, mercy, and guidance will stay close to us in our future and that You would help us to always remember that You have a plan for us. That we are only a small part of Your great story. Amen."

With tears forming in her eyes Bree had added her own "amen."

She had worn the same gown from their first wedding. She had tried to part with it on many occasions but was so very grateful she hadn't been able to do that. Grant was dressed in her favorite attire for him; jeans and a flannel shirt, sleeves rolled up to the elbow, of course, and hiking boots. Though they were hidden by her gown, Bree, too, was wearing her favorite hiking boots.

Glory agreed to be the maid of honor and had shown up at the church with a beautiful bouquet of yellow roses mixed with a few colorful wildflowers that were still holding on, daring winter to come.

"Grant told me these were your favorite," Glory said as she gave Bree a fierce hug. The two had worked out any issues that might have been standing in the way of their friendship once Grant and Bree had talked through all that had taken place. Bree knew Grant had never intentionally deceived her, even as Vic.

Pa and Cal had fought, playfully, about who would give the bride away. Cal and Annie had brought the kids and were losing the battle every few minutes of trying to keep them in the church rather than running through the field just outside. In the end Pa won the fight to be Bree's escort. Cal had finally given in, but with concessions.

"Okay, Pa. You can have this honor," Cal told the old codger. "But I get first dibs on the toast once we get back to your house."

Pa was happy to make that concession. He had walked Bree down the aisle as though she was his most prized possession. When he handed her off to Grant, there were tears in both his and Ma's eyes. Bree handed a perfect yellow rose from her bouquet to Ma, who was seated on the front pew, and gave Pa a kiss on his wrinkled cheek as he placed her hand in Grant's.

Bree thought the ceremony was even more magical than the first time she and Grant had said their vows almost eight years before. At that ceremony there had only been acquaintances since neither she nor Grant had any family still living. She had been so happy to be marrying Grant, it hadn't mattered at the time.

Looking around the church as she had said her vows, Bree saw smiles and some tears on the faces of all the people God had brought into her life in the few years she was without Grant. Rather than leaving her to suffer alone, God had sent support through friends who had become like family. Even Sam, the night security guard and her now trusted new friend, had made the hour long drive from Knoxville to celebrate with the couple.

Bree felt tears coming again. As she looked into Grant's eyes she saw that he wasn't totally composed either. His mouth moved and only she knew the silent words he uttered.

"I love you, Little Lady."

As if she needed any more reasons to let the tears flow, that had done it. Bree was sure she had never experienced a happier day in her life.

She and Grant had agreed to have the preacher read from Jeremiah and Ecclesiastes during the ceremony rather than the typical wedding verse about love from I Corinthians.

"These two standing before us have woven a most unusual story as God brought them together, not once, but twice," said the pastor friend of Ma and Pa's. "They have each chosen a verse they both feel applies to their lives."

He read from Jeremiah 29:11. *"'For I know the plans I have for you, declares The Lord, plans to prosper you and not to harm you, plans to give you hope and a future.'"*

He immediately followed with Ecclesiastes 4: 9-12. *' "Two are better than one, because they have a good return on their labor; If either of them falls down, one can help the other up. Also, if two lie down together, they will keep warm. But how can one keep warm alone? Though one may be overpowered, two can defend themselves. A cord of three strands is not quickly broken."'*

Before Bree knew it, the preacher was finished. "What God has joined together, once again, let no man part. I now pronounce you husband and wife. You may now kiss your bride."

And kiss her he had. Bree still got shivers when she thought about that kiss. It had continued on through the cheers and applause from the audience until the pastor had cleared his throat, repeatedly, to get their attention. Even so, Grant had pressed his face against her neck and inhaled deeply of her scent before letting her go.

"I'll never get enough of that," he had told her.

Since that moment, both had said daily, almost hourly, prayers of thanks to God for reuniting them.

Grant had spent countless hours handling the legalities of his name change both personally and with his companies. Once he had gotten that straightened out, he had sold off a couple of the smaller businesses to pay back the insurance money, with interest, that Bree had received when he had legally been declared dead.

They had merged Mountain Sky Productions with Smoky Beauties to form Smoky Mountain Sky. Inc. Financially they were still in great shape, thanks to smart investing on both their parts.

Once Brannon had recovered and been proven as a suspect in the assaults on Bree, he had been taken into custody and charged with assault. He was also looking at a charge of attempted murder for putting Grant in the hospital after the wreck. At his hearing, Grant and Bree had testified with the truth, but had also spoken in kindness adding a plea to the judge for leniency toward Brannon. He was now back in a mental hospital where he could get proper treatment rather than standing trial with a possible conviction that could have landed him serving time in a state penitentiary.

Both Grant and Bree felt that with most legal decisions out of the way they could finally begin their lives together for the second time.

Once the sky faded, they moved to the opposite porch on the east side of the cabin where the setting in front of them was every bit as beautiful as the sunset they had witnessed. Grant had been out of the hospital for three weeks and was fully recovered. He took a seat in the oversized swing he had made himself. Opening his arms, he beckoned Bree to his lap. She readily accepted the offering. Grant pressed his face into her neck, inhaling her lavender scent.

"This is my most favorite place in the world," he told her between breaths.

Bree was well aware he was referring to her nape as well as their home. He had certainly told her often enough. Knowing how well he loved the fragrance, she kept an ample supply of her signature lavender lotion close at hand and used it often.

In between kisses, they watched as the sky slowly turned from a lingering rosy glow to midnight blue and a beautiful full moon began to rise. Neither one moved or spoke; they barely even breathed as they watched for the phenomenon that they knew in their hearts was going to take place.

Within a few minutes they smiled at what they were witnessing and turned to each other for a passionate kiss. As always, Grant's kisses left her breathless.

"I can't think of a more perfect time to attempt to conceive our son than during a blue sky at night, Bree, my love." Grant told her between kisses.

"It would be a lovely story to tell our *daughter*," she replied, kissing him back.

Laughing his bear of a laugh, Grant stood and carried Bree into their bedroom.

"And I couldn't agree more that tonight would be the perfect time to make that attempt," she told him.

And they proceeded to do just that.

# Author's Note

Thank you for your interest in Grant and Bree's story. "Blue Mountain Sky" is the first book in the Smoky Mountain Mist series. As with any book involving the area of the Great Smoky Mountains, food is a required part of the story. At least that is my belief.

I have enclosed the recipe for Ma's Cathead biscuits after this note. Books two and three in this series are in the works. "Red Morning Glory" due to be released in the fall of 2016, and "Dawn's Gray Light" will also include recipes from one of the characters in the books.

I hope you enjoyed this book and soon enjoy the biscuits. I would love to hear from you either way. Please contact me via email at cyntaylor2016@gmail.com.

# Recipe for Ma's Cathead Biscuits
*(made in the true mountain fashion)*

Pre-heat oven to 400°.

Sour 2 cups milk by stirring in 1 teaspoon white vinegar or use buttermilk if you have it. I never seem to when I want to make biscuits.

Mix approximately 2 1/2 cups self-rising flour and 1/2 teaspoon salt with about 1/2 cup lard (Crisco). I use a whisk on the flour first to make fluffier biscuits. If substituting vegetable oil for lard use about 1/2 cup. This actually makes lighter biscuits. And it's healthier. But mountain folk don't really care.

Pour milk into flour mixture and stir with a large spoon until consistency reaches a thick dough. The dough should cling to the spoon and should be just a bit difficult to drop off. Add more milk if necessary. This is a trial and error method.

Scoop large rounded spoonfuls onto greased baking pan or stone. Place IMMEDIATELY into pre-heated oven.

Bake for 15-20 minutes until baked through and browned to liking.

The biscuits get their name because when baked they are flat and look similar to a cat's head. No cats were harmed during the development of this recipe.

Serve with butter and homemade apple butter. (Apple Butter recipe available in the third book of the Smoky Mountain Mist series, "Dawn's Gray Light")

Enjoy.

Read on for an excerpt
from the second book
in the Smoky Mountain Mist series
"Red Morning Glory."

# Red Morning Glory

Instead of trying to catch the other bikers, Glory should have been paying closer attention to the road conditions. The Cove had lots of areas where the creek crossed over the road. This was no problem in a car but a bike was a different story.

Glory was massaging her head again, wondering why the pounding wouldn't go away and was in fact, continuing to worsen. She never heard the Hager twins coming up behind her. By the time Glory realized that what she was peddling through was more mud than water, it was too late.

The twins had pulled up on each side of her. Six tires hit the mud at once. The mud flew up and hit her. She was so startled she lost control of the bike and ended up on all fours, elbow deep in mud, as the twins sped off laughing.

Strong arms were there almost instantly to help her up. She wiped the mud from her eyes and looked up into the laughing face of Tanner Slade. Where had he come from so quickly? Groaning inwardly Glory wondered how much worse this day could possibly get.

"Didn't you hear me, Red?" He was asking. "I tried to warn you they were coming up behind you."

In between laughter, Tanner was telling her she needed more experience if she was going to tackle a road of this caliber. He was pushing her hair out of her face and trying to wipe the tip of her nose with a handkerchief while trying to get his laughter in check. That was disgusting. Who knew where that handkerchief had been?

"Don't you dare touch me with that. And get your hands off me you...you...vagabond."

Glory was shivering now from the chill in the early morning air mixed with the mud and water. She was angry at herself for being caught in this position and angry at Tanner Slade for laughing at her.

"Vagabond?" Tanner gave her a serious questioning look. "Now why on earth would you call me that? You don't even know me. As a matter of fact, do you even know what a vagabond is?"

"Of course I do. I am not an idiot and you are the very image of one," Glory told him through chattering teeth. Why in the world had Grant and Bree thought this guy would be someone she could be interested in?

Tanner wasn't sure if she was still calling him a vagabond or if he had been moved into the category of idiot. He grabbed her shoulders as if to chastise her further just as Bree and Grant rode up.

"Hey guys. What happened here?" Grant asked, giving Tanner an accusatory stare as he took in Glory's disheveled condition.

Tanner loosened his hold but not before he felt a long shiver run through Glory's body. "You're freezing," He accused her. Glory had no time to answer before Grant yelled at Tanner.

"Slade, what did you do to her?" Grant was approaching now looking every bit like the bear most people thought he was. Bree grabbed his arm to restrain him as she whispered in his ear. He stopped instantly.

Ignoring Grant, Tanner quickly removed his lightweight jacket to wrap it around Glory's shoulders. She wasn't surprised that it didn't seem to bother him the jacket was going to get all muddy.

The church van pulled up at that moment. Without further comment, Slade picked her up and carried her to the vehicle. He deposited her gently on the seat next to the teenage girl Glory had chastised only minutes before. He gave the driver instructions to take the next gravel road and pulled the door closed before heading back to his bike. Glory saw him speak briefly with Grant and Bree. The three of them mounted their bikes and started up the road.

"Miss Donaghan, what happened to you? Did someone ride too close to you too?"

The two teens, or four teens, Glory wasn't quite sure, were questioning her at the same time. Her mouth felt like cotton, her teeth were chattering too badly for her to answer and she was certain her head was going to explode. The van was behind the three bikers. Glory barely saw the gravel road before they turned onto it. She was sure she would never have seen it had she not heard Tanner tell the driver to take it. And why was she seeing everything in pairs?

Wow, she was beginning to feel hot. Probably from embarrassment. She hated being seen by her youth group as weak. This definitely wouldn't boost her expertise in their eyes. And wait until the congregation heard what a lousy job she had done today as chaperone. Yes, today would almost certainly end her career as church youth director. A thought, that two months ago would have made her very happy, was having the opposite effect now. And Tanner Slade. What right did he have to come up and take over like that?

And why did her head feel like it weighed a hundred pounds? She was suddenly so sleepy...and dizzy. She wondered for a moment what had been in that mud. Maybe she was really Super Girl in disguise and allergic to what must have been kryptonite mud. Wouldn't that be funny?

But Super Girl was a blonde, wasn't she? And if she was Super Girl shouldn't she be able to fly? She laughed, thinking flying might be fun and she should fly away right now. She jumped up and opened the van door to do that. Good thing the van had already stopped and Tanner Slade was there to catch her. Instead of flying up she fell down into his arms.

Glory looked into his eyes and saw compassion. But she also saw something else that closely resembled disgust. Well that was fine with her. She didn't like the man anyway. She began struggling to escape his arms but it was as though a steel vice held her captive.

Glory shook her index finger in his face. "Let me go or I will make you regret it."

"And how do you plan to do that?" Tanner asked, almost smiling.

"I am Super Girl and I have skills!" Glory announced, right before her world went dark. Had Tanner not been holding her, her face would have met mud once again.

If you loved **Blue Mountain Sky**, check out the other romance novels from Mantle Rock Publishing.

**Irish Encounter** - After almost three years of living under a fog of grief, Ellen Shepherd is ready for the next chapter in her life. Perhaps she'll find adventure during a visit to Galway. But the adventure awaiting her includes an edgy stranger who disrupts her tea time, challenges her belief system, and stirs up feelings she thought she'd buried with her husband.

Before writing novels, Hope Toler Dougherty published non-fiction articles on topics ranging from gardening with children to writing apprehension.

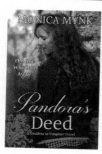

In **Pandora's Deed** Savannah Barrett fled her Dreyfus home to escape bullies, planning to stay away for good. Body image struggles have led to a life of empty relationships. Can former tormentor, Geoff Spencer be the man to love her anyway?

Monica Mynk writes young adult fiction that encourages spiritual principles in her Goddess to Daughter Series. The second book, **Medusa's Hands** is also available.

**A Most Precious Gift** - Dinah Devereaux, New Orleans-born slave and seamstress, suddenly finds herself relegated to a sweltering kitchen, though never cooked a day in her life. When she accidentally burns the freedom papers of Jonathan Mayfield, her fear of the fields becomes secondary.

Jaqueline Freeman Wheelock draws on her southern roots to create to create this intriguing love story.

Mantle Rock Publishing
www.MantleRockPublishing.com

If you loved **Blue Mountain Sky**, check out the other romance novels from Mantle Rock Publishing.

**Keeper of Coin** shares the struggles of the Carty sisters as they immigrate from Ireland to St. Louis. Will sixteen year old Anne be able to save the funds needed to bring her siblings safely to a new life?

Author Mary Kay Tuberty shares the letters from her family that lay the framework for this wonderful series of three historical romances. The second novel in the series, **Keeper of Trust** is available.

**A Light in Bailey's Harbor** takes the reader to Wisconsin in the 1880s where Kate Kippling struggles with taming her abundant personality. New lighthouse keeper, Blake Strawberry causes Kate to question her faith.

Bethany Baker writes a heart-warming romance in the lakeside Wisconsin town of Bailey's Harbor.

**Callie's Mountain** brings the struggles of 1790s living in the East Tennessee Mountains to life. Callie finds herself in a marriage arranged by her father which makes her life in a new area more difficult.

Katt Anderson sheds light on prejudices in rural areas. The second novel in the series, **Susannah's Hope** is also available.

Mantle Rock Publishing
www.MantleRockPublishing.com